Prais

"A brilliantly written and
uncomfortable undercurrent of modern day horror... so honest and ....
than even readers unfamiliar with Cushing will find this an extremely
powerful read" **HellBound Times**

"Possibly the most touching tale that we have had the privilege to
review... *Whitstable* effortlessly blurs reality and fiction in a beautifully
realised tale of good versus evil... A must read; not only for fans of
Cushing but lovers of great writing in general" **Geek Syndicate**

"The sensitivity, technical virtuosity and razor-sharp wit of the author's
storytelling make *Whitstable* an entertaining, emotionally resonant and
insightful read... Stephen Volk is at the top of his game... An
enthusiastic salute to a towering figure in British cinema, a perceptive
exploration of the link between imagined and experienced horror, and
one of the most gripping and original stories you'll read this year"
Andy Hedgecock (co-Fiction Editor, Interzone)

"Stephen Volk has produced a novella that works both as a gripping
thriller and as a beautiful and heart-breaking tribute to one of horror's
finest stars... Very few books have actually caused tears to well up in my
eyes. The love and respect that the author has for Peter Cushing is laid
bare on the pages, and as a reader you cannot help but become totally
immersed in this poignant tale" **Jim McLeod, Ginger Nuts of Horror**

"Elegant, moving and absolutely magnificent" **Simon Kurt Unsworth**

"Peter Cushing was my first hero, and in my opinion Stephen Volk has
done something heroic by putting the man who fought onscreen monsters
at the heart of a very human drama. Sad, tinged with a palpable sense of
loss, beautifully written, and blessed with an unerring eye for crucial
detail, *Whitstable* is a story to savour. If I may be so bold, I'm convinced
that Peter Cushing would have approved" **Gary McMahon**

"A wonderful piece" **David Pirie, author of *A Heritage of Horror:
The English Gothic Cinema***

"I loved *Whitstable*! It's a beautiful love letter to a man, a genre, and an
era that means so much to those of us of a certain age"
Mick Garris, producer, *Masters of Horror*

Whitstable

Stephen Volk

Spectral
Visions

spectralpress.wordpress.com

A SPECTRAL PRESS PUBLICATION

PAPERBACK ISBN: 978-0-9573927-2-4

First edition, May 2013

Printed by Lightning Source, Milton Keynes.

Editor/publisher Simon Marshall-Jones

Layout by Neil Williams

Cover art by Ben Williams © 2012

Spectral Press, 5 Serjeants Green, Milton Keynes, Bucks, MK14 6HA

Website: *spectralpress.wordpress.com*

CONTENTS

Smile for the camera.

Old Saying

He couldn't face going outside. He couldn't face placing his bare feet into his cold, hard slippers. He couldn't face sitting up. He couldn't even face opening his eyes. To what? The day. Another day without Helen in it. Another day without the sun shining.

For a moment or two before being fully awake he'd imagined himself married and happy, the luckiest man on earth, then pictured himself seeing her for the first time outside the stage door of the Theatre Royal, Drury Lane: she a shining star who said a platypus looked like "an animal hot water bottle"—he in his vagabond corduroys, battered suitcase, hands like a Dürer drawing, breath of cigarettes and lavender. Then as sleep receded like the waves outside his window, he felt that dreadful, dreaded knot in his stomach as the awareness of her no longer being there—her non-presence—the awful, sick emptiness, rose up again from the depths. The sun was gone. He might as well lie there with his eyes shut, because when his eyes opened, what was there but darkness?

Habitually he'd rise with the light, drink tea, take in the sea view from the balcony, listen to the wireless and sometimes go for a swim. He did none of these things. They seemed to him to be activities another person undertook in a different lifetime. *Life. Time.* He could no more picture doing them now than he could see himself walking on the moon. The simplest tasks, the very idea of them, seemed mountainous. Impossible.

Yet it was impossible, also, to lie there like a dead person, greatly as it appealed to do so. It was something of which he knew his darling would so disapprove, her reprimand virtually rang in his ears and it was this that roused him to get up rather than any will of his own.

His will was only to...

But he didn't even have the strength for that.

She was his strength, and she was gone.

Helen. Oh, Helen...

Even as he sat hunched on the edge of the bed, the burden of his loss weighed on his skinny frame. He had no choice but to let the tears flow with the same cruel predictability as his dream. Afterwards, weaker still, he finally rose, wiping his eyes with now-damp knuckles, wrapping his dressing gown over baggy pyjamas and shambling like something lost and misbegotten towards the landing. A thin slat shone between the still-drawn curtains onto the bedroom wallpaper. He left the room with them unopened, not yet ready to let in the light.

A half-full milk bottle sat on the kitchen table and the smell hit him as soon as he entered. The sink was full to the brim, but he poured the rancid liquid in anyway, not caring that it coated a mound of dirty plates, cups, saucers and cutlery with a viscous white scum.

He opened the refrigerator, but it was empty. He hoped the milkman had left a pint on the doorstep: he hated his tea black. Then he remembered why he had no groceries. Joycie did it. Joyce, his secretary, did everything for "Sir". He pictured again the hurt in her eyes when he'd told her on the telephone she would not be needed for the foreseeable future, that she needn't come to check that he was all right because he *was* all right. He'd said he needed to be alone. Knowing that the one thing he didn't want to be was alone, but that was not the way God planned it.

Nasty God.

Nasty, nasty God...

He shut the fridge. He didn't want food anyway. What was the point? Food only kept one alive and what was the point of that? Sitting, eating, alone, in silence? What was the point of that?

He put on the kettle. Tea was all he could stomach. The calendar hung facing the wall, the way he'd left it.

The letter box banged, startling him, shortly followed by a knock on the wood. It was Julian the postman, he thought, probably wanting to give his condolences in person. He held his breath and had an impulse to hide. Instead he kept quite still. Julian was a sweet chap but he didn't want to see him. Much as he knew people's wishes were genuine, and appreciated them, his grief was his own, not public property. And he did not want to feel obliged to perform whenever he met someone from now on. The idea of that was utterly repellent. How he dealt with his inner chasm, his utter pain and helplessness, was his own affair and other people's pity or concern, however well-meaning, did not make one iota of difference to the devastation he felt inside.

He stood furtively by the doorway to the hall and watched as a package squeezed through and fell onto the welcome mat, and beyond the glass the silhouette of the postman departed.

It had the unmistakable shape of a script.

His heart dropped. He hoped it was not another one from Hammer. He'd told them categorically via his agent he was not reading anything. He knew Michael had newly found himself in the chair as Managing Director, and had a lot on his plate, but could he really be so thoughtless? Jimmy was a businessman, but he also counted him a friend. They all were. More than friends—family. Perhaps it was from another company, then? Amicus? No. Sweet Milton had his funny American ways, but would never be so callous. Other companies were venal, greedy, but not these. They were basically gentlemen. They all knew

Helen. They'd enjoyed laughter together. Such laughter, amongst the gibbets and laboratories of make-believe. Now, he wondered if he had the strength in his heart to meet them ever again.

He picked up the package and, without opening it, put it on the pile of other unread manuscripts on the hall stand. Another bundle sat on the floor, a teetering stack of intrusion and inconvenience. He felt no curiosity about them whatsoever, only harboured a mild and uncharacteristic resentment. There was no small corner of his spirit for wonder. They were offers of work and they represented the future. A future he could not even begin to contemplate. Why could they not see that?

He sighed and looked into the mirror between the hat hooks and what he saw no longer shocked him.

Lord, the make-up job of a master. Though when he sat in the make-up chair of late he usually had his hairpiece to soften the blow. Never in public, of course: he abhorred that kind of vanity in life. Movies were different. Movies were an illusion. But—fifty-seven? He looked more like *sixty*-seven. What was that film, the part written for him but one of the few he turned down? *The Man Who Could Cheat Death.* But he couldn't cheat death at all, could he? The doctors couldn't, and neither could he. Far from it.

Dear Heavens...

The old swashbuckler was gone now. Fencing in *The Man in the Iron Mask*. The Sheriff of Nottingham. Captain Clegg of Romney Marsh... He looked more like a Belsen victim. Who was it said in a review he had cheekbones that could cut open letters? He did now. Cheeks sucked in like craters, blue eyes sunk back in deep hollows, scrawny neck, grey skin. He was positively cadaverous. *Wishful thinking*, he thought. A blessing and a curse, those gaunt looks had been his trademark all these years, playing cold villains and erudite psychopaths, monster-hunters and those who raised people from the dead. Yet now the only person he desperately craved to bring back from the grave he had no power to. It was the one role he couldn't play. Frankenstein had played God and he had played Frankenstein playing God. Perhaps God had had enough.

The kettle whistled and the telephone rang simultaneously, conspiring to pierce his brain. He knew it was Joycie. Dear Joycie, loyal indefatigable Joycie, who arrived between dry toast and correspondence every day, whose concern persisted against all odds, whose emotions he simply couldn't bear to heap on his own. He simply knew he could not speak to her, hear the anguish in her voice, hear the platitudes even if they weren't meant as platitudes (what words could *not* be platitudes?) and, God knows, if he were to hear her sobs at the end of the line, he knew it would tip him over the edge.

Platitude:

An animal that looks like a hot water bottle.

Hearing Helen's laughter, he shut his eyes tightly until the phone stopped ringing, just as it had the day before. And the day before that.

Quiet loomed, welcome and unwelcome in the mausoleum of his house.

He stared at the inert typewriter in the study, the signed photographs and letter-headed notepaper stacked beside it, the avalanche of mail from fans and well-wishers spilling copiously, unattended, across the floor from the open bureau, littering the carpet. He pulled the door shut, unable to bear looking at it.

Hardly thinking what he was doing, he re-entered the kitchen and spooned two scoops of Ty-phoo into the tea pot and was about to pour in boiling water when he froze.

The sudden idea that Joyce might pop round became horrifically possible, if not probable. She wasn't far away. No more than a short car journey, in fact, and she could be here and he would be trapped. Heavens, he could not face that. That would be unbearable. Instantly he realised he had to get out. Flee.

Unwillingly, sickeningly, he had no choice but to brave the day.

Upstairs he shook off his slippers, replacing them with a pair of bright yellow socks. Put on his grey flannel slacks, so terribly loose around the waist. Needing yet another hole in the belt. Shirt. Collar gaping several sizes too big now, too. Tie. No time for tie. Forget tie. Why was he forced to do this? Why was he forced to leave his home when he didn't want to? He realised he was scared. The scaremonger, scared. Of *this*. What if he saw somebody? What if they talked to him? Could he be impolite? Unthinkable. Could he tell them how he really felt? Impossible. What then?

He told himself he was an actor. He would *act*.

Back in the hall he pulled on his winter coat and black woollen hat, the kind fishermen wear, tugging it down over his ears, then looped his scarf round his neck like an over-eager schoolboy. February days could be bright, he told himself, and he found his sunglasses on the mantelpiece in the living room sitting next to a black and white photograph of his dead wife. At first he avoided looking at it, then kissed his trembling fingertips and pressed them gently to her cheek. His fingerprints remained on the glass for a second before fading away.

***

He walked away from 3 Seaway Cottages, its curtains still drawn, giving it the appearance of a house in slumber. As a married couple they'd bought it in the late fifties with money he'd earned from *The Hound of the Baskervilles*, because having a place by the sea—especially here, a town they'd been visiting for years—would be good for Helen's breathing. "You have two homes in life," she'd said, "the one you're born in and another you find," and this one they'd found, with its big, tall windows for painting under the heavens and enjoying the estuary views across Shell Ness, clapboard sides like something from a whaling port in New England. They were blissfully happy here, happier than either of them could have dreamed Now it seemed the house itself was dreaming of that happiness.

He paused and breathed in deeply, tasting brine at the back of his tongue.

Good, clean fresh air for her health.

The mist of his sighs drifted in short puffs as he trudged along the shingle, patchy with errant sprigs of grass, in the direction of the Neptune pub, the wind buffeting his fragile frame and kicking at the ends of his dark, long coat. Above him the sky hung Airfix blue, the sky over a cenotaph on poppy day, chill with brisk respect, and he was small under it.

Automatically he'd found himself taking the path he and Helen had taken—how many times?—arm in arm. Always arm in arm. His, muscular and taut, unerringly protective: hers light as a feather, a spirit in human form, even then. If he had grasped and held her, back then... stopped her from... *Stupid. Foolish thoughts.* But his thoughts at least kept her with him, if only in his heart. He was afraid to let those thoughts be blown away. As he placed one foot in front of the other he felt that stepping from that path would be some sort of blasphemy. That path was his path now, and his to tread alone.

His heart jumped as he noticed two huddled people coming towards him, chequered green and brown patterns, their scarves fluttering. A man and wife, arm in arm. He felt frightened again. He did not want to see their faces and fixed his eyes past them, on the middle distance, but in his peripheral vision could tell they had already seen him and saw them look at each other as they drew unavoidably closer. His chest tightened with dread.

"Mr Cushing?"

He had no alternative but to stop. He blinked like a lark, feigning surprise. Incomprehensibly, he found himself smiling.

"Sorry." The man had a local accent. "Bob. Bob and Margaret? Nelson Road? I just wanted to say we were really sorry to hear about your wife."

He took Bob's hand in both of his and squeezed it warmly. He had no idea who Bob was, or Margaret for that matter.

"Bless you."

The man and woman went on their way in the direction of West Beach and Seasalter and he walked on towards the Harbour, still smiling. Still wearing the mask.

He was an actor. He would act.

Act as if he were alive.

***

The sky had turned silver grey and the wind had begun whipping the surface of the water. After passing the hull of the *Favourite*, that familiar old oyster yawl beached like a whale between Island Wall and the sea, he sat in his usual spot near Keam's Yard facing the wooden groynes that divided the beach, where he was wont to paint his watercolours of the coast. But there was no paint box or easel with him today. No such activity could inspire, activate or relax him and he wondered if that affliction, that restless hopelessness, might pass. If it meant forgetting Helen, even for an instant, he hoped it would not.

Usually the music of the boats, the flag-rustling and chiming of the rigging, was a comfort. Today it was not. How could it be? How could anything be? When there was nothing left in life but to endure it?

He took off his sunglasses and pulled a white cotton glove from his pocket onto the fingers of his right hand, momentarily resembling a magician, then lit a John Player unfiltered. It had become a habit during filming: he said, often, he didn't want to play some 'Nineteenth Century Professor of the Nicotine Stains'. As he smoked he looked down at his bare left hand which rested on his knee, lined with a route-map of pronounced blue veins. He traced them with his finger tips, not realising that he was enacting the gentle touch of another.

He closed his eyes, resting them from the sun and took into his smoker's lungs the age-old aroma of the sea. Of all the senses, that of smell more than any other is the evoker of memories: and so it was. He remembered with uncanny clarity the last time he and Helen had watched children building 'grotters'—sand or mud sculptures embellished imaginatively with myriads of oyster shells—only to see the waves come in and destroy them at the end of a warm and joyful Saint James's Day. Clutching his arm, Helen had said, "Such a shame for the sea to wash away something so beautiful." He'd laughed. His laughter was so distant now. "Don't worry, my dear. They'll make more beautiful ones next year." "But that one was special," she'd said, "I wanted that one to stay."

The fresh salt air smarted in his eyes.

"I know who you are," said a disembodied young voice.

Startled, he looked up and saw a boy about ten years old standing at an inquisitive distance, head tilted to one side with slats of cloud behind him and a book under his arm. He and Helen had no children of their own, or pets for that matter, but felt all the children and animals in the town were their friends. He remembered talking to the twins next door and asking what they wanted to be when they grew up—clergyman, sailor—and them innocently turning the question back at him, albeit that he was already in his fifties: *What do* you *want to be when you grow up?* Good question, for an actor. But this one, this boy, he didn't recognise at all.

"You're Doctor Van Helsing."

The man's pale blue eyes did not waver from the sea ahead of him.

"So I am."

The boy threw a quick glance over his shoulder, then took a tentative step nearer. He wore short trousers, had one grey sock held up by elastic and the other at half-mast. Perhaps the other piece of elastic had snapped, or was lost.

"I... I saw what you did," he stammered eagerly, tripping over his words, but they nevertheless came ten to the dozen, a fountain. "You... you were powerful. He escaped back to his castle and he... he leapt up the stairs four, five, six at a time with his big strides but you were right behind him. You were *determined.* And you couldn't find him, then you *could.* And he was about to go down the trapdoor but he saw you and threw something at you and it just missed and made a really big clang, and then he was on top of you squeezing the life out of your throat and it hurt a really lot..." The boy hastily put his book between his knees and mimed strangulation with fingers round his own neck. "He had you down on the floor by the fireplace and you couldn't breathe he was so strong and mighty and you went like this—" His eyes flickered and he slumped. "And he was coming right down at you with his pointed teeth and at the last minute you were awake—" The youngster straightened his back. "And you pushed him away and he stood there and you stood there too, rubbing your neck like this. And he was coming towards you and your eyes went like *this*—" He shot a glance to his left. "And you saw the red curtains and you jumped up and ran across the long, long table and tore them down and the sunlight poured in.

And his back bent like this when it hit him and his shoe shrank and went all soggy and there was nothing in it. And he tried to crawl out of the sunlight and you wouldn't let him. You grabbed two candle sticks from the table and held them like *this*—" He crossed his forearms, eyes blazing, jaw locked grimly. "You forced him back and his hand crumbled to ashes and became like a skeleton's, and he covered his face with his hand like this, and all that turned grey and dusty too, and his clothes turned baggy because there was nothing inside them. And everything was saved and the sign of the cross faded on the girl's hand. And after you, you—*vanquished* him, you looked out of the coloured window at the sky and put your woolly gloves back on. And the dust blew away on the air."

Indeed.

The man remembered shooting that scene very well. The old 'leap and a dash' from the Errol Flynn days. Saying to dear old Terry Fisher: "Dear boy, I seem to be producing crucifixes from every conceivable pocket throughout this movie. Do you think we could possibly do something different here? I'm beginning to feel like a travelling salesman of crosses." He'd come up with the idea himself of improvising using two candle sticks. He remembered the props master had produced a duo at first too ornate to work visually, but the second pair were perfect.

"That was you, wasn't it?"

"I do believe it was," Peter Cushing said.

He did not look at the boy and did not encourage him further in conversation, but the youngster ventured closer as if approaching an unknown animal which he assumed to be friendly but of which he was nevertheless wary, and sat on the wall beside him squarely facing the sea.

The man was now patting his jacket pockets, outside and in.

"What are you looking for?" The boy was curious. "A cross? Only you don't need a cross. I'm not a vampire."

"I'm very glad to hear it. I was looking for a photograph. I usually have some on me... I really don't know where I've put them..."

"A what?"

"A photograph. A signed one." No response. "Of yours truly." Still no response, puzzlingly. "Isn't that what you'd like?"

"No," the boy said, sounding supremely affronted, as if he was dealing with an idiot.

"Oh..."

"I want to ask you something much more important than that. *Much* more important."

"Oh. I see."

Cushing looked around in a vain attempt to spot any parents from whom this child might have strayed, but there were no obvious candidates in evidence. If the boy *had* got lost, he thought, then it might be best for him to keep him quietly here at his side until they found him, rather than let him wander off again on his own. He really didn't want this responsibility, and he certainly didn't want company of any sort, but it seemed he didn't have any choice in the matter.

"I said I'm not a vampire." The boy interrupted his thoughts. "But I know somebody who is. And if they get their own way I'll become one too, sooner or later. Because that's what they do. That's how they create other vampires." The child turned his head sharply and looked the man straight in the eyes. "You said so."

Quite right: he had done. It wasn't hard to recall rewriting on set countless scenes of turgid exposition on vampire lore so that they didn't sound quite so preposterous when the words came out of his mouth.

"Who is this person?" Cushing played along. "I probably need to take care of him, then."

"He's dangerous. But you don't mind danger. You're *heroic*."

Cushing twitched an amused shrug. "I do my best."

"Well it *has* to be your best," the boy said with the most serious sense of conviction. "Or he'll kill you. I mean that."

"Then I'll be as careful as possible. Absolutely."

"Because if he finds out, he'll hurt you, and he'll hurt me." The words were coming in a rapid flow again. "And he'll hurt lots of other people as well, probably. Loads of them." The boy drew up his legs, wrapped his arms round them tightly and tucked his knees under his chin. His eyes fixed on the horizon without blinking.

"Good gracious," Cushing said. "You mustn't take these type of pictures too much to heart, young man."

"Pictures? What's *pictures* got to do with it?" The abruptness was nothing short of accusatory. "I'm talking about *here* and *now* and you're the vampire hunter and you need to *help* me." The boy realised his harsh tone of voice might be unproductive, so quickly added, sheepishly: "Please." Then, more bluntly, with an intense frown: "It's your *job*."

It's your job—Vampire Hunter.

You're heroic.

You're powerful.

Cushing swallowed, his mouth unaccountably dry.

"Where's your mother and father?"

"It doesn't matter about them. It matters about *him*!"

The boy stood up—and for a second Cushing thought he would sprint off, but no: instead he walked to a signpost of the car park and picked at the flaking paint with his fingernail, his back turned and his head lowered, as he spoke.

"My mum's boyfriend. He visits me at night time. Every night now. He takes my blood while I'm asleep. I know what he's doing. He thinks I'm asleep but I'm not asleep. It feels like a dream and I try to pretend it isn't happening, but afterwards I feel bad, like I'm dead inside. He makes me feel like that. I know it. I can't move. I'm heavy and I've got no life and I don't want to have life anymore." He rubbed his nose. His nose was running. Bells tinkled on masts out of view. "That's what it feels like, every time. And it keeps happening, and if it keeps happening I know what'll happen, I'm going to die and be buried and then I'll rise up out of my coffin and be like him, forever and ever."

Something curdled deep in Cushing's stomach and made him feel nauseous. He obliterated the pictures in his mind's eye—a bed, a shadow sliding up that bed—and what remained was a bleak, dark chasm he didn't want to contemplate. But he knew in his heart what was make believe and what was all too real and it sickened him and he wanted, selfishly, to escape it and pretend it didn't exist and didn't happen in a world his God created.

He felt a soft, warm hand slipping inside his. *Helen?* But no. It belonged to the little boy.

"So will you?"

"Will I what?" In a breath.

"Will you turn him to dust? Grey dust that blows away like you did with Dracula?"

"Is that what you want?"

The boy nodded.

Oh Lord... Oh God in Heaven...

Cushing stared down without blinking at the boy's hand in his, and the boy took his expression for some sort of disapproval and removed it, examining his palm as if for a splinter or to divine his own future. The man suddenly found the necessity to slap his bony knees and hoist himself to his feet.

"Gosh. You know what? I'm famished. What time is it?" His fob watch had Helen's wedding ring attached to its chain: a single gold band, bought from Portobello Road market when they were quite broke. The face read almost twenty past eleven. "There's a shellfish stall over there and I think I'm going to go over and get myself a nice bag of cockles." He straightened his back with the aid of his white-gloved hand. "I do like cockles. Do you like cockles?"

The boy, still sitting, did not answer.

"Would you like a bag of cockles? Have you ever tried them?" He took off the glove, finger by finger.

The boy shook his head.

"Do you want to try?"

The boy shook his head again.

"Well, I'm going to get some, and you can try one if you want, and if you don't, don't."

***

The boy observed the old man closely as he flicked away the tiny cover of the shell with the tip of the cocktail stick and jabbed the soft contents within.

"Will you put a stake through his heart?"

Cushing twirled it, pulled it out and offered the titbit, but the boy squirmed and recoiled.

"You know, long, long ago, people believed in superstitions instead of knowing how the world really worked." He popped the tiny mollusc into his mouth, chewing its rubbery texture before swallowing. "They didn't know why the sun rose and set and what made the weather change, so sometimes they thought witches did it. And because they thought witches might come back and haunt them after they were dead, they'd bury them face down in their graves. That way, when they tried to claw up to the surface they'd claw their way down to Hell instead. But, you know, mostly superstitions are there to hide what people are really afraid of, underneath."

"You know a lot. You're *knowledgeable*," the boy said, happy to have his presumptions entirely confirmed. "But you have to be. For your occupation. Vampire Hunter."

Cushing had had enough of the taste of the cockles. In fact, he hadn't really wanted them anyway. He wrapped the half-empty tub in its brown paper bag, screwed up the top and deposited it in the nearest rubbish bin a few feet away. Whilst doing so, he scanned the car park, again hoping to see the errant parents. "Do you see him in mirrors? Does he come out in daylight? Because that's how I discover whether someone is a vampire or just someone human that's *mistaken* for a vampire, you see."

"He does go out. In the day time, but..."

"Aha. What does that tell you?"

"Different ones have different rules. Sometimes they *can* be seen in daylight like in *Kiss of the Vampire* on TV. You weren't in that one, so you don't know. There are different sorts, like there are different cats and dogs but you can put a stake through their heart. That *definitely* works, always. And that's what you're brilliant at."

Cushing sat back down next to the boy, put on his single white glove and lit another cigarette. He remembered something that had troubled him in his own childhood. He'd mistakenly thought the Lord's prayer began: *Our Father who* aren't *in Heaven*. But if God *wasn't* in Heaven, where was He? The question, which he dared not share even with his brother, had kept him awake night after night, alone. Where? He rubbed the back of his neck: a gesture not unfamiliar to fans of Van Helsing.

"I know what you're thinking," the boy said. "You're thinking how to trap him."

"No. I'm not."

"What are you thinking then?"

"Do you want me to tell you, truthfully? Very well. I believe if there's something troubling you at home, whatever it is and however bad it is, the best thing to do—the first thing to do—is to tell your mother."

The boy laughed. "She loves him. *She* won't believe me. *Nobody* will. That's why I need *you*."

"Perhaps your mother wants to be happy."

"Of *course* she does! But she doesn't want to be killed and have her blood sucked all out, does she?"

"This man might be a good man trying his best. I don't know him, but why don't you give him time to prove himself to you and I'm sure you'll accept him for what he is."

"I *know* what he is! He won't change. He *won't*! Vampires don't become nice people. They just stay what they are—evil. And they keep coming back and coming back till you stop them!"

"Listen. I'm being very serious..."

"I know. You're *always* serious."

"Yes, well. These feelings you have about your mum's new boyfriend?..." Peter Cushing felt cowardly and despicable, and even as he was uttering the words disbelieved them almost entirely, but did not know what else to say. "They'll go away, in time. You'll see. They'll pass. Feelings do."

"*Do* they though? Bad feelings? Or do they just *stay* bad?"

Cushing found he could not answer that. Even with a lie.

"My mum wants to marry him. She loves him. He's deceived her because really he doesn't love her at all. He just wants to suck *her* blood, too."

"But you have to understand. I can't stop him."

"Why?"

Cushing stumbled for words. Fumbled for honesty. "I don't know how. You have to talk to somebody else. Somebody..."

"Yes you do! You *do*! The villagers are in peril, and *I'm* in peril, and you're Doctor Van Helsing!"

A large seagull landed on the rubbish bin and began jabbing its vile beak indiscriminately at the contents.

"I'm sorry. I'm—"

"Yes, you *can*. Please! *Please!*..."

But Cushing could say no more. Dare say no more. The desperation in the boy's voice struck him mute and the rolling eye and the hideous ululating of the seagull made him look away. He felt pathetic and cruel and lost and selfish and small—but he wasn't responsible for this child. Why should he be ashamed? The vast pain of his own grief was heavy enough to bear without the weight of another's. Even a child's. Even a poor, helpless child's. He was an actor, that was all. Van Helsing was a part, nothing more. All he did was mouth the lines. All he did was be photographed and get his angular face blown up onto a thirty-foot wide screen. Why was the responsibility his? Who asked this of him, and why shouldn't he say no?

Now a second gull, even bigger, had joined the first and added to the cacophony. In a flurry of limbs they squawked and spiked at the bag the cockles were in, then began snapping at each other in full scale war with the yellow scissors of their horrid, relentless maws.

When their aggression showed no sign of abatement, Cushing crushed out the remains of his cigarette on the stone, hurried over and shooed them away with flailing arms from the debris they were already scattering with their webbed feet and flapping wings. He felt their putrid dead-fish breath poisoning his nostrils. They coughed and gurgled defiantly and showed their pink gullet-holes before begrudgingly ascending.

After stuffing the brown paper bag deeper into the bin he turned back, and to his sudden alarm saw the boy walking briskly away.

"Wait."

But the boy did not wait.

Where were the parents? Where were the dashed parents and why were they not—? ...but all Cushing's thoughts and recriminations hung in the air, incomplete and impotent. He had denied the boy the help he had craved—however fantastical, however heartfelt, however absurd—and now the lad was gone.

"Wait..."

Cushing sat back down, alone, and saw that the book from under the boy's arm was still sitting there.

***

Movie Monsters by Denis Gifford.

He placed it with its cellophane-wrapped cover on the desk of the public library. They knew him well there. They knew him well everywhere, sadly, and he intuited as he approached that there was an unspoken choreography between the two female assistants, vying for who would serve him and who would be too busy. It was not callousness that made them do so, he knew— merely the all-too-British caution that a wrongly-placed word might cause unnecessary hurt. Did they realise their shared eye contact alone caused hurt anyway? He forced a benign smile.

"Good afternoon."

"Good afternoon, Mr Cushing." The younger one drew the short straw. He was still unshaven, had been for days and he wondered if he looked rather tramp-like. Little he could do about it now.

"I'm terribly sorry to trouble you, my dear, but I wonder if you might help me? I found this library book near Sea Wall today and I wonder if you'd be so kind as to tell me the name and address of the person it belongs to. They must be dreadfully worried about losing it. I'd be most awfully grateful."

"By all means. Just a moment, sir..." She checked the date stamped inside the cover and turned to consult the

chronologically-arranged index of book cards behind her. Her
rather thick dark hair fell long and straight across her shoulder
blades. She wore a tight green cardigan and high heels that made
her calves look chunky from behind, and he pondered whether
she was happily married and, if so, for how long. With how many
years ahead of her? "That's fine, Mr Cushing. We'll make sure
he knows his book has been returned."

"No, you see—bless you—it's no trouble for me to return it
to him personally. I really am quite grateful for the distraction."

A flicker in her eyes. "Oh. I understand. Of course. In that
case..." She coughed into her hand and looked at the details a
second time. "The name is Carl Drinkwater." She read out in full
an address in Rayham Road. "That's one of the new houses over
on the other side of the Thanet Way, off South Street. Do you
know it?"

"Not at all."

She opened a drawer and produced a small map of the town,
unfolded it and marked the street with a circle in red Biro as the
black one was empty.

"Splendid. Thank you so much." He took her hand and kissed
it, as was his habit ("immaculate manners; such a gentleman")
before walking to the exit.

"Mr Cushing?" He turned. "Mrs Cushing, sir. I'm so very
sorry. She was such a delightful woman."

He nodded. "Thank you so much."

He was astonished to hear the four words come from his
throat, because the fifth would have stuck there and choked him.
He hoped the woman was married and happy, with children and
more happiness ahead of her. He truly did.

***

He returned home to fetch his bicycle, the Jaguar of more
joyful days secreted in the garage these many months: memories

preserved in aspic, too painful to be given the light of day. He swapped his woollen fisherman's hat for a flat cap, grabbed a heavier scarf, and, with the library book in his pannier, rode via Belmont Road and Millstrood Road to the boy's house—what appeared to be a two-bedroom bungalow on the far side of the railway track.

The February sun was low by now and the sky scrubbed with tinges of purple and ochre. He chained his cycle to a lamp post opposite and stayed in the protective shadow between an overgrown hedge and a parked white van (*For All Your Building Needs*) as he scrutinized the place from afar.

The garage had a green up-and-over door with a dustbin in front of it on the drive. The lawn grass was thin and yellowing. He could see no garden ornaments and the flatness of the red brick frontage was broken only by a plastic wheel holding a hosepipe fastened to the wall. Two windows matched, a third didn't and the door, frosted glass and flimsy, was off-centre.

He looked at his watch—Helen's ring tinkled against the glass face—and placed it back in his pocket. He blew into his hands, preparing himself for a long wait, hoping he had enough cigarettes left in his packet and, no doubt because of the worry this engendered, lit one, no doubt the first of many. He might of course smoke the lot and find this turned out to be a fruitless enterprise. There was no guarantee the man went out on a Saturday night, though a lot of men normally did. He was not dealing with, perhaps, the most normal of men.

After fifteen minutes or so a dog-walker in a quilted "shortie" jacket passed and Cushing pretended he was mending a puncture with his bicycle pump, never more conscious that his acting had to be as naturalistic as possible. Believability was all. The Labrador sniffed his tyres but the dog-walker, who resembled the sports commentator Frank Bough, yanked the lead and progressed on his way with only the most cursory of nods.

Cushing fixed his bicycle pump back into place and looked over at the house.

Hello. The light was on in the hall now, beyond the frosted glass. Shapes were donning coats. The door opened. He ducked down behind the white van, craning round it to watch a man in a donkey jacket tossing his car keys from hand to hand, a few steps behind him a boy in a football strip following him to a parked Ford Zephyr. Reflections in the windscreen stopped him from getting a good look at the man's face.

Cushing quickly hid in case Carl, whose eyes were on the road ahead, saw him. He listened for the engine to start and waited for it to sufficiently fade away.

As soon as it had, he crossed the road and knocked on the front door. He could hear the television on inside, so rapped again slightly harder. "All right, all right, keep your hair on..." A woman approached the glass and he could already make out she wore a red and white striped top, a big buckle on a wide belt and bell-bottomed jeans.

The door opened to reveal someone who, he imagined, thought herself attractive and feminine but who seemed to have endeavoured to make herself anything but. Her hair was drastically pulled back from her forehead in a pony tail, her clothes did nothing to enhance her figure, and there was nothing graceful or pretty in her demeanour or stance. He thought of the quiet perfection of Helen by comparison and had to quickly dismiss it from his mind. He reminded himself of his abiding belief that all women should be respected and accorded good manners at all times.

He took off his flat cap. "Mrs Drinkwater?"

"Yeah."

"You don't know me..."

"Yeah, I do."

His eyebrows lifted. "Oh?" Was she a fan of Hammer films, then, like her son?

"Of course I do. I've seen you on the telly."

Fool. He'd been the BBC's Sherlock Holmes over a number of televised adventures alongside Nigel Stock as Dr Watson. Naturally she recognised him. His portrayal of the great detective, after all, had been widely acclaimed.

"Morecambe and Wise," the woman said.

Oh dear, he thought. How the mighty are fallen. Serve him right. The Greeks had a word for it: *hubris*. The sin of pride.

"You live round here," she said.

"That's quite correct. My name's Peter Cushing."

He extended a hand, which the woman saw fit to ignore.

"I know."

"May I come in, please? It's about your son Carl."

"What about Carl? What's he done now? I'll kill him."

"Nothing. Absolutely nothing, Mrs Drinkwater. Nothing wrong." He showed her the copy of *Movie Monsters* which he'd tucked under his arm. "I found this library book of his and I'm returning it, you see."

She took the book off him and looked at it but didn't move or speak, even to say thank you.

He said again, equally politely: "May I come in?"

More from being taken unawares than hospitality, the woman stepped back to allow him to enter. He cleaned his shoes on the mat while she walked back into the room with the television on, without asking him to follow her. Though his own manners were faultless, he refused to judge others on their inadequacy in that area. It was often down to their upbringing, he believed, and that could not be their own fault. We are all products of our pasts: none more so than he himself. Some said he was stuck in it. Another, unwanted, era. But he merely believed politeness and courtesy between human beings was a thing to be valued, in any era. Treasured, actually.

The ironing board was out and she was making her way through a pile of washing, which she resumed, clearly not about to interrupt her workload on his account. She did not offer him a cup of tea or coffee and did not turn down the TV, but simply carried on where she'd left off, half-way through a man's shirt, tan with a white collar, Cliff Richard's variety show the activity's accompaniment. The ceiling was textured with Artex swirls, the fireplace with its marble-effect surround boarded up with a sheet of unpainted hardboard, and a patio door led to a garden enclosed by fencing panels.

He saw a recent edition of the *Radio Times* lying on the arm of the sofa, its cover announcing the introduction of a new villain into the *Doctor Who* pantheon. Dear old Roger Delgado looking as if he'd stepped straight from a Hammer film with his widow's peak and black goatee. He thought of Jon Pertwee's dandyish Doctor compared to his own "mad professor" saving the Earth from the invading hordes of soulless Daleks. He thought how easy it was to save the world, and how hard, in life, to save...

"Why d'you want to talk about him?"

"It was Carl who chose to talk to me, in fact. May I?" He noted she seemed confused by the question, so sat himself on the sofa anyway, his voice having to compete with Cliff Richard's. "It was curious, very curious indeed. You see, he approached me earlier today confidently believing I was *actually* Doctor Van Helsing, the character I played in the Dracula films for Hammer several years ago." He chuckled. "Many years ago, actually. How time flies..." He noticed a stack of books on the cushion next to him: *The Second Hammer Horror Films Omnibus* with Christopher Lee on its orange cover offering his bare chest to a victim, *The Fifth* and *Seventh Pan Books of Horror Stories*, the

Arrow paperback editions of *Dracula* and *The Lair of the White Worm*. "I see he's a fan..."

"Monster mad. I wish he wasn't. Not healthy if you ask me. None of it."

He smiled. "Dear lady, that's my bread and butter you're talking about. For my sins."

She didn't match his smile and still didn't turn down the television.

He loosened his scarf. The gas-effect electric fire was cranked up and the skin on his neck was beginning to prickle.

"Carl loves you very much, Mrs Drinkwater." He chose his words carefully. "He cares an awful lot about what happens to you. The more he was talking to me, it was very clear he felt you were in danger. And he was in danger too. Very much so."

She grunted, straightening her back then slamming down the iron and running it back and forth up the sleeve. "He's got an active imagination. Always did, always will. Got his bloody father to thank for that. Telling the kid those stories of his— ghosts, goblins, monsters—scaring him, keeping him awake. What do you expect?"

"I don't think stories hurt people, Mrs Drinkwater. Not really hurt."

"How do you know?" She set the iron on end with a thump. Rearranged the garment roughly. "Have you got children?"

"No. Sadly." He and Helen had not been blessed in that way.

"Then you haven't sat up with them crying and hugging you. Over stories. Or anything else for that matter, have you?"

"That's very true."

"So you don't know anything about it, do you?"

"No, I don't. You're quite right. But..." He gazed down at the carpet and noticed he was still, rather ridiculously, wearing his bicycle clips. He reached down and took them off, idly playing with them as he talked, as if they were a cat's cradle or a magic trick. "But what he said concerns me. I'm sorry. You must understand, surely? Children don't say things without reason."

"Don't they? Kids can be cruel. You lead a sheltered life, you do. Kids can get at you in ways you wouldn't even dream of. If they think you deserve it."

"Can they?"

The iron hissed. "You should hear what I get in the ear every day. Dad this, Dad that."

"He idolizes his father."

"Yeah, the father who sneaked him into the cinema to see that *Dracula* you're so proud of when he was eight years old. Oh yeah. Bought a ticket, pushed the bar of the emergency exit, let him in. Like the teddy boys or mods do. To an X film. His <u>son</u>. Don't tell me that helped any problems he had in school or anywhere else, because it didn't. He was scared to death of the world before that and, you know what? It made him *more* scared. That's why he's playing silly buggers."

Peter Cushing rubbed his eyes. Dare he ask the question? He was compelled to. He had come here. He would never forgive himself if he didn't.

"Do excuse me for asking this, but has your boyfriend ever... ever raised his hand to Carl? Hurt him in any way?"

"No." The woman cut into his last word. "Les loves that boy."

Loves.

"How long have you known him?"

"Long enough." She stiffened. "Why?"

He loves that boy.

"As I say... Carl seemed, well, I have to be honest, Mrs Drinkwater... troubled."

"Well there's nothing troubling him in this house, I tell you that for nothing. It's all in his bloody mind." The shirt flicked to and fro, the iron hitting it repeatedly like a weapon of violence. She turned her body to face him, hand on hip. "Why do you make those horrible films anyway? Eh?"

"To be truthful I hate the term 'horror film'. Car crashes and the concentration camps and what's happening in Northern Ireland, that's horror. I think of the fantasies I star in as fairy tales or medieval mystery plays for a new generation. If you take the 'O' from Good and add a 'D' to Evil, you get God and the Devil—two of the greatest antagonists in the whole of history. And Van Helsing is important because he shows us Good triumphs. After all, Shakespeare used horrific images in *Titus Andronicus*, and mankind's belief in the supernatural in *Macbeth*, and nobody belittles the fellow for that. I think the best so-called 'horror' shows us our worst fears in symbolic form and tries to tell us in dramatic terms how we can overcome them."

"Yeah, well." Her face, turning back to the ironing board, betrayed an ill-concealed sneer. "I didn't pass enough exams to understand all that. We didn't have books in our house. My dad was too busy working."

He sighed. "Mrs Drinkwater, I'm quite sure you don't want this discussion and neither do I. Please just put my mind at rest, that's all I ask. Truly. Just talk to Carl. Listen to him."

"You've listened to him. Do you believe him?"

"My dear, I'm just an actor. It's his mother he should talk to."

"Or a psychiatrist."

"If that's what you genuinely think."

"It's no business of yours what I think."

"You're quite right, of course." He stood up, putting his bicycle clips in his pocket. "Perhaps I shouldn't have come, but please believe me when I say I did so only out of concern for Carl. I apologise profusely if I've upset you. That wasn't my intention at all."

"You haven't upset me," she said.

"I'm sorry for disturbing you. I'll see myself out."He thought the conversation was over but he'd barely reached the door to the hall before she said behind his back:

"Why don't you make nice, *decent* films, eh?"

He turned back with sadness, both at the slight and his own ineffectiveness. He knew she felt accused and belittled by his very presence, undermined by his unwanted interference and presumptions and posh voice and good manners and wanted to attack it, all of it.

"Don't you think I've got enough problems with him, without this...? Without him talking to strangers...? Talking rubbish...?"

His blue eyes shone at her.

"I can't believe he's saying what he's saying, honest to God. He's got no business to." Her cheeks were flushed now, voice quavering on the edge of losing control. "I swear, Les is good as gold with that kid. Better than his real dad, by a mile. You want to know who *really* hurt him? If you want to know the truth, his *father* did. He did that by buggering off. And there isn't a day goes by I don't see that in my son's eyes, so don't come here accusing me or anybody else when the real person isn't here anymore." He could see she fought away demons, the worst kind—and tears.

Instinctively, he walked over and took her hands in his. "I beseech you, my dear. Talk to your son."

Appalled, she backed away from him.

"I don't need to talk to my son."

She reached the wall and couldn't back away any further. His face was close to hers and he looked deeply into her eyes, his own vision misty, almost unable to get out the words he must.

"My dear, dear girl. I've lost someone I loved. Please don't do the same."

She snatched away her hands as if the touch of him was infectious.

"How fucking *dare* you!" She shoved him in the chest. Then shoved him again. "Get out of here." He staggered backwards, feeling it inside the drum of his old, brittle ribs. "Get out of my fucking house! Get *out*!"

Gasping for breath and words, he stumbled to the front door as she berated him with her screams and obscenities and later remembered nothing of getting to his bicycle or getting from Rayham Road to Seaway Cottages except that he had to stop a number of times to wipe the tears from his eyes and by the time he got indoors a thin film of ice had formed covering his cheeks.

***

A film played in the darkened theatre of his brain. A Hammer film, but not their usual fare. Not set in Eastern Europe in the nineteenth century, but in Canada in the present, even though it was filmed at Bray. The opening shot of darling Felix Aylmer, who'd played his father in The Mummy, ogling two young girls through binoculars. A vile creation. A 'dirty old man' in common parlance—hideously inadequate euphemism that it was.

"He made us play that silly game…"

Square-jawed Patrick Allen as the father. *"If he touched her, I'll kill the swine!"* Gwen Watford, an actress who always appeared to be on the verge of tears. *"You expect me to be objective when a man has corrupted my daughter?"*

Corrupted. Precisely.

He knew many films where the house outside town harboured inconceivable evil, and had starred in quite a few where the villagers marched up to it demanding justice or revenge, but in this picture fear has the upper hand. The family is powerful. The hero, weak. The community knows how old Mr Olderberry "can't keep his eyes off children", but the townsfolk choose to keep their heads firmly in the sand. Even the police think it must be the girls' own fault.

The child's own fault.

The very concept was odious. As odious as the sight of gummy old Felix pursuing the girls through the woods, staggering like Boris Karloff after the one in pigtails, stepping over the overturned bicycle. Wordlessly pulling the rowing boat containing the two children back to shore by its slimy rope…

***

A girl sat up in the tree and it didn't seem at all peculiar but it worried him. It was an oak tree, old and sturdy, with deeply wrinkled bark. The little girl didn't seem distressed but she did seem determined, a strong-willed little soul. She wore a frilled collar like a Victorian child and he thought she was clutching a toy or teddy bear but couldn't make it out clearly through the leaves and branches. "Come down," he called to her. He looked around but there was no-one else about. Only him. So it was down to him to do something. "Come down." But the girl wouldn't come down. She just looked down at him, frowning seriously. "Come down. Please," he begged. But still she didn't move. A man came along. A man he didn't know. The man said to him: "What are you doing?" He couldn't answer. He got confused, he didn't know why, but before he could answer anyway, the man stepped closer and went on: "You know exactly what you're doing don't you? Don't you?" Rage and aggression built up in the man's face and his tightly pursed mouth extended to became a vicious-looking yellow beak. And this beak and another beak were prodding and poking at a boy's short trousers, snatching and tearing out gouts of underwear. The underwear was made of paper. Newspaper. And somehow he was upset that what was written was important, the words were important.

He woke to the sound of seagulls snagging and swooping above his roof.

At the best of times, he despaired at their racket. And these were not the best of times. Now the noise was no less than purgatory. As a child in Surrey he'd thought they were angels, but now he held no illusions about the species. The creatures were the very icon of an English seaside town, but they were relentless and without mercy. He'd once seen a large speckled gull going for a toddler's bag of chips, almost taking off its fingers, leaving it bawling and terrified in its mother's embrace. They were motivated by only selfish need and gratification, thought only of their own bellies and their own desires. It seemed almost symbolic that we never ate sea birds, knowing almost instinctively that their insides would be disgusting, inedible, rank, rancid, foul. It seemed to Cushing that their screeching was both a bombastic call to arms and a cry of pain.

He sat up, finding himself on the living room sofa.

He looked at the clock and saw it was four o'clock. Since it was sunny beyond the drapes, he deduced it must be four o'clock in the afternoon. He was still in his pyjamas and dressing gown and still too tired to care.

He'd hardly slept a wink all night. In fact, the short, shallow period of sleep broken by the dream had been by far the longest. Perhaps an hour. The rest, when he could, had been spent at most in a fitful doze, and that only occasionally, interspersed as it was with shambling wanders round the house or up and down stairs in the dead of night. That darkness inculcated fears was a truism, but such knowledge did nothing to abate it. Fears multiplied as he'd curled up wide-eyed, turning circuitous thoughts over in his mind, multiplying still more while he'd walked aimlessly from room to room, in a futile search for distraction, illumination, resolution or peace of mind. All evaded his grasp.

He had lain in his bed thinking of Carl Drinkwater lying in his. The boy's words, the whole encounter, replayed in his ears. What did he hear? Was he misguided? Did he take it all at face value when he shouldn't have? Was the mother right? All kinds of doubts set in. Most of all, that he was mentally accusing a man he'd never met of the most despicable act, the vilest *crime* imaginable—based upon what?

He had woken, walked round like a penitent, unable to sleep, as these questions went round and round in his head. Who was he to pronounce? Who was he to judge? Who was right? Who was wrong? Who was good? Who was evil? He wished he could talk to somebody, but who would listen to the silly gibbering of a recently bereaved man whose very job was spinning a preposterous yarn and making it seem true?

It was Sunday but he didn't want to go to church. Too many people. Too many eyes. In fact he hadn't been to church since Helen's funeral. Afterwards the young vicar at St Alphege's had told him: "If you ever want to come and talk, Peter, for any reason, you know where I am." He'd said: "My name's Godfrey. You can call me God." Then he had nudged Peter's arm with his elbow. "I'm joking." Peter didn't want to hear a joke and he didn't want to laugh. He didn't want to go back for a chat with 'God' either. 'God' could find other people to chat to. He'd rather have a good actor like Peter Sallis or Miles Malleson playing a vicar than that young fake who was acting the part anyway. As Olivier had said, "Be sincere, dear boy, always be sincere—and when you've faked that, you've cracked it."

But if you cannot do good, he thought now, where *is* God? Where?

Unable to turn without a painful reminder confronting him— the furniture was all Helen's choice from her favourite antiques dealer, and every piece of it held a story—he dragged his feet up to his studio, the 'playroom', at the top of the house. For five or ten minutes he sat and gazed up through the windows along one wall at the darkening sky above. The far table was strewn with art supplies, palettes rainbowed with dried paint and uncapped tubes of aquamarine and burnt sienna gone hard as concrete. The miniature theatre sets he'd made to the original Rex Whistler designs sat like frozen moments of time waiting patiently to be awakened. Model aeroplanes dangled on fishing line, Lancaster bomber, Spitfire, Messerschmitt: a veritable Battle of Britain suspended in the air. Frozen in time, like he was in so many ways. A child with his toys. A boy playing at being a man. What was a 'play' anyway but 'playing'? He thought of Captain Stanhope in *Journey's End*, the part he never got a chance to do. In glass-fronted cabinets the length of the room stood hundreds of model soldiers, the British Army through the ages: the Scots Greys at Waterloo; Desert Rats at El Alamein; Tommies at Normandy. In days gone by he'd get them out and solve international problems on his knees on the carpet. His men were clever, bold, indefatigable, strategic, victorious—always. But they were no use to him now. They'd fought all those battles, but what could they do to fight this one? Now they were as useless and impotent as he himself. He suddenly wanted to give the boy all those toy soldiers. He wanted to give him all the toys in the world.

Helen gazed out at him radiantly from a pastel drawing pinned to the wall.

He slid a record out of its sleeve, placed it on the gramophone and slumped in the threadbare rocking chair letting Symphony Number One by Sibelius wash over him. It always had the effect of reminding him of the wonder of human achievements, the humility with which we should revere, in awe, such pinnacles of artistic endeavour, but it struggled to do that now. He cast his mind back to being on set singing Giuseppe's song from *The Gondoliers* to Barbara Shelley, competing with Chris Lee to see who could sing the nightmare song from *Iolanthe* fastest without missing a word. He tried to think of singing and old friends laughing, whilst knowing a child somewhere wept into its pillow.

The door bell rang.

He opened his eyes. Rather than lift the needle and risk scratching the LP, he let the music play as he went downstairs to answer it.

A figure stood outside in the dark. He could make out the distinctive square shoulders and upturned collar of a donkey jacket. He could see no face, just a man's outline and the collar-length hair covering his ears backlit by the almost iridescent purple of the night sky. He had not replaced the light bulb in the conservatory, which had blown weeks ago, nor had he switched on the hall light in his haste to open the front door. Now he wished he had done both.

"Mr Cushing?" It was a light voice and one he didn't recognise, or had reason to fear, but some part of him tightened.

"Yes?"

Instinctively, Cushing shook the extended hand—calloused, dry as parchment from physical work, not the hand of a poet: an ugly hand—and gazed into the face of a man in his thirties with sand-blond, almost flesh-coloured hair and beard. *Thirty three*, the older man thought, peculiarly, unbidden. The age Jesus was when he died: *Thirty-three*. The long hair and beard was 'hippie'-like, the style of California's so-called 'flower children', but now ubiquitous, of course. Under the donkey jacket Cushing saw a red polo-neck jumper and blue jeans, flared, faded in patches from wear—a working man, then. No. He corrected himself from making any such assumption: threadbare jeans were, inexplicably to him, the fashion of the day. Students at Oxford wore jeans. Jeans told him nothing.

"Hello, mate. My name's Les Gledhill…"

Les loves that boy.

"First of all, I've got to say I've always been a massive fan of your films. I know, I know probably everyone says that. You probably get bored with hearing it. But I really mean it, sir. I feel quite nervous talking to you, in point of fact…" Realising he had not released the actor's hand, the man now did so, laughing and holding his hands aloft, pulling faces at his own crassness and ineptitude.

Les loves that boy.

Cushing didn't ask himself how the long-haired man had found his address. Everyone in town knew where its most famous resident lived—though most conspired in respecting his privacy.

Les loves that boy.

"Sorry. Sorry. Am I disturbing you? Only, it's really important I have a word." The visitor rubbed his hands together vigorously in the night air, hopping from foot to foot. "I, ah, think there's been a misunderstanding. A really, really *big* misunderstanding, mate…" he chuckled, "and I really, really want to clear it up before it goes any further." Still laughing, he pointed both index fingers to the sides of his head, twirling them in dumb-show semaphore for the craziness of the situation.

"I'm so sorry to be a bore…" Cushing's voice retained its usual mellifluous charm. "It's Sunday evening. This isn't a very good time, to be perfectly honest. In fact, I'm expecting guests any minute…" On tip-toes he craned over the other man's shoulder, pretending to be scanning the path beyond.

"This won't take long. I promise to God. Just a minute of your time, mate. If that. Honestly…"

"I have food in the oven. I'm most terribly..." Blast. The pyjamas and dressing gown were a giveaway that he was lying, and he had to think fast. "I'm, I'm just about to get changed. This really isn't convenient. If you'll excuse me..." He did an excellent job also of covering up the fact that his heart was pounding thunderously. *When you can fake that, dear boy...*

A hand slapped against the door. "Sorry, mate. Hold on. Hey. *Mate...*"

It stopped the door from closing but Gledhill, almost immediately embarrassed by his brisk action, quickly removed it and stuffed it in his jacket pocket, laughing again.

"Listen. Please. I really, *really* want to clear this up, sir. I swear, you have no idea what this is doing to me. You, a respected man in this, this community, I mean, *loved* in this town, let's face it, Christ, thinking..." One cheek winced as if in momentary pain. "When she... that's why I had to come over, see. I couldn't let..."

Cushing wondered why he still felt afraid. Much as he hated to admit it, the man seemed reasonable. Why did he *hate to admit* it? What had he *presumed* the chap would be like? Here he was. Not an ogre. Perplexed, certainly. Bewildered, genuinely. It seemed. And—unless a consummate actor himself—shaken. The voice didn't sound angry or vicious in the least, or beastly. Or *evil*—that was the remarkable thing. It sounded confused, and quite upset. No—*hurt*. Terribly hurt. Devastated, in fact.

"Of course, if you're busy, sir, I understand. Blimey, I have no right to just barge over here, knock on your door, expect you to..." Running out of words, the man in the donkey jacket backed away, then turned to go. Then, as he reached the white-painted garden gate, turned back. "Look, the truth is... I'd hate you to think I'd done anything to hurt that boy. Or whatever you think. That's just... Just not the case. Truly." He made one last, haltering plea. "I… I just wanted to explain to you you've got the wrong end of the stick, that's all. That's what concerns me, more than anything. You're a decent man. A perfect gentleman. You don't need this. It's not fair." The front door had not shut and, this being so, he took this for some kind of invitation and walked quickly back into the conservatory.

Peter Cushing's fingers did not move from the latch on the inside of the door. "I'd rather we discuss it here, if we must."

Gledhill stopped, suddenly bowed his shaggy head and plunged his ruddy, working man's hands deep in his jacket pockets, shuffling. "Yes, of course, mate. No problem."

Letting the front door yawn wider in a slight act of contrition, Cushing retraced his steps and switched on the hall light, then returned to stand on the welcome mat whilst the man in the donkey jacket hovered in silhouette at the mercy of the shrill wind cutting in from the sea. It buffeted the door, sending an icy breath though the house, room to room, riffling paperwork like a thief.

Picked out of the darkness by the paltry spill of light from the hall, Gledhill shook a solitary Embassy from its packet. "Listen." He rubbed one eye. "Carl is a good kid, a great kid. He's quirky, a laugh, in small doses, don't get me wrong. He's a character. But he has problems, that's what you don't realise." The lighter clicked and flashed, giving a splash of illumination from his cupped hand to his chin and upper lip. "He says things. Things that aren't true." A puff of smoke streamed from the corner of his mouth. "All the bloody time. Not just about me. About everybody. The school already has him down as a liar. And a bully. They have problems with him. He hurts other kids. That's what kind of child he is, Mr Cushing. His mother worries about him day and night. So do I. Day and night."

Night.

Cushing remained tight-lipped. The face of a hundred movie stills. Immobile. "You're telling me I shouldn't believe a word that comes out of his mouth."

"Honest to God." The man's next exhale was directed at the moon. The whites of his eyes seemed flesh-coloured too, now. Perhaps it was the ambient yellow glow from within. He dawdled in its penumbra. "You think he's some kind of angel? You don't know him. You don't know any of us." He let that fact, and its obvious truth, bed down in Cushing's mind. "I didn't have to take on this woman with her boy, did I? Let's face it, lots of blokes would run for the hills the minute they know there's a kid in tow. And I haven't, have I? Because I love her. I'm trying to piece this family together. God knows. I'm going to marry her, for Christ's sake. Put everything right for both of them. The boy too. I'm not a bad person." He offered the palms of his hands.

"Then what do you have to fear from me?" Cushing spoke quietly and with precision.

"I don't know." Gledhill shrugged. "I don't know *what* you think."

And he laughed again. And the laugh had a *wrongness*. There was something in it, a grace note, deep down, disingenuous, that the older man detected and didn't like. If pressed, he couldn't have explained it any more than he could have explained why, on meeting his wife he knew instantly they were meant to spend the rest of their lives together: it wasn't even love, it was that he'd met his *soul*. Similarly, the thing embedded in Les Gledhill's laugh was inexplicable, and, inexplicably, *enough*.

"I think you'd better leave now. Good night to you."

He shut the door but found something wedged into the jamb, preventing it from closing. The laughter had stopped. He didn't want to look down and didn't look down, because he knew what he would see there: A foot rammed in between the bottom of the door and the metal footplate.

O, Lord. O, Jesus Christ.

"I'm trying to be reasonable. I'm trying to..." Gledhill's teeth were clenched now, tobacco-stained, his face only inches from the other man's. "Why are you doing this?"

"I beg your pardon?"

"Why are you *doing* this?" The Kent accent had become more pronounced, transforming into a Cockney harshness. "I've done nothing to you. I'm a total stranger to you. Have you ever met me before? No. So why are you doing this to me? Going to my house, upsetting my girlfriend. I come home to find her in bits. How d'you think that makes me feel? Before I know it she's firing all kinds of questions at me. Stupid questions. *Ridiculous* questions—"

"Please..." The older man's voice was choked with fear. He couldn't disguise it any more. It took all his strength to hold the door in place. "I have nothing more to say."

Gledhill's face jutted closer still, his shoulder firm against the door, holding it fast, and Cushing could detect the strong sweet reek of—*what, blood, decay?*—no, alcohol on the man's breath. But something else too. *Something of death.* "What kind of person are you, eh?"

Cushing stood fast, half-shielded by the door, half protected, half vulnerable. "I was going to ask you exactly the same question. Except Carl answered that for me. In his own way."

"How? What did he say?"

"He said you're a vampire."

The laugh came again, this time a mere blow of air through nose and mouth accompanied by a shake of the head, then the bubbling cackle of a smoker's hack. It came unbidden but there was no enjoyment behind it or to be derived from hearing it.

"That kid cracks me up. He really does. Such a joker. You know what? That's hilarious." The turn of a word: "*You're* hilarious." Now Gledhill's expression was deadly serious. "You're being hilarious now."

"That doesn't mean I can't stop you."

"I'm innocent! I've done *nothing* wrong. Haven't you been listening to a bloody *word* I've said? You need to clean your ears out, mate. Get a hearing test, at your age. Pay attention to people. Not just listen to idiots."

"Carl isn't an idiot. I don't consider him an idiot."

"I know you don't." One elbow against a glass panel of the door, Gledhill jerked his other arm, tossing his spent cigarette into a flower bed without even looking where it fell. "Why do you believe him and not me, eh? What gives *you* the right to cast judgement on *me*, anyway? You, a stupid film star in stupid films for stupid people."

So much for being a lifelong fan. His true colours, at last. "I know evil when I see it."

A grunt. "What? Dracula and Frankenstein and the Wolf Man?"

"No. I'm talking about the true evil that human beings are capable of."

"And what's that, eh? Tell me. Tell me what's going on in your *sick* mind, because I have no bloody idea."

Cushing did not reply. Simply stared at him and with supreme effort refused to break his gaze. He saw for the first time that the monster's eyes were as colourless as the invisibly pale eyebrows that now made an arch of self-pity over them.

"You think I'd hurt him? I wouldn't hurt a hair of his head. Cross my heart and hope to die." With the thumb of one hand, Gledhill made the sign of the cross, horizontally across his chest, then from his chin to his belly.

"It's curious," Cushing said, one hollow cheek pressed to the side of the door. "In vampire mythology, evil has to be invited over the threshold. And she invited you in, didn't she? With open arms."

"Yeah, mate. It's called love."

"Love can be corrupted. I will not be witness to that and let it pass."

"How Biblical." The glistening eyes did not suit the sneer that went with them.

"I have been a Christian all my life. It gives me strength."

"You Bible-thumpers see evil everywhere."

"No, we don't. But to God innocence is precious. It's to be valued above all things. It must be protected. Our children must be safe. It's our duty as human beings."

"Too right. They *do* need to be protected," the creature that was Gledhill said. "From old men talking to young boys on the beach. Boys all alone. What did you say to him, eh? That's what the police are going to ask, don't you think, if you go to them?" His voice fell to a fetid, yet almost romantic, whisper. "That's what people are going to ask. What were they talking about, this old man who lives all alone? This old man who makes horrible, sadistic films about cruelty and sex and torture, someone who's never had any children of his own, they tell me, someone who *adores* other peoples' children? This old man and this innocent little boy?"

His skin prickling with the most immense distaste, Cushing refused to be intimidated, even though the nauseous combination of beer and cigarette breath in the air was quite sickening enough. "I'm quite aware he is innocent, Mr Gledhill. And I'm quite aware what you might say against me."

"Good. And who do you think they'll believe, eh? Me or you?"

"They'll believe the truth."

"Then that's a pity. For you," the mouth said. It wasn't a face any more. Just an ugly, obscene mouth.

Cushing did nothing to back away. He knew that once he did that, physically and mentally, he was lost. But he was backing away in his mind like a frightened rabbit, and he feared that Gledhill could see it in the clear rock pools of his eyes. Frightened eyes.

"I should knock you into next week," Gledhill breathed. "Just the thought of what you were doing, or trying to do, makes me want to puke, d'you know that? But I'm not someone who takes the law into their own hands. I obey the law, me. I'm a law-abiding..."

Though he wanted to cry out, Cushing stood his ground. He was resolute, even if he didn't feel it. He felt crushed, battered, clawed, eviscerated. The truth was, he knew, if he gave into impulse and stepped away, then he was afraid that would mean *running* away. And what might follow that? His visitor was clearly big enough and strong enough to barge through a door held by a flimsy old man with no effort whatsoever. Yet he hadn't. Why, the old man dared not contemplate. Sheer *inability*, not bravery, glued him to the spot. But how much of that could the other eyes looking back at him see?

"You need to drop this, I'm telling you," Gledhill said. "For your own good, all right? I'm doing you a favour coming here. You don't get it, do you?"

"Oh, I do. I 'get it' entirely. Thank you for clarifying any doubt in my mind."

Cushing instantly wished he'd kept that thought to himself, but now there was no going back and he knew it.

With all his strength he shoved the door hard in the hope the latch would click and he'd turn the key in the Chubb to double-lock it before Gledhill got a chance to push from his side—but Gledhill had already pushed back, and harder. He was a builder, labourer, something—*heathen*, Cushing didn't know why that word sprang to mind, but he didn't want him in his house, he wasn't a reader he was a destroyer of books, and people. He fell back from the door, panting, a stick man, brittle. Then he did decide to run, the only thing he could do as it flew open, banging against the wall.

He dashed to where the telephone and address book sat on the hall table and snatched up the receiver and put it to his ear, swinging round to face the man in the doorway as his finger found the dial.

To his astonishment Gledhill stopped dead, his feet see-sawing on the threshold, his boots pivoted between toe and heel.

"Sorry! Sorry. Sorry. I'm really sorry, mate! I shouldn't have talked to you like that. Shit! That, that's the booze talking. I don't normally get like that. I don't normally say boo to a fucking goose, me." The swear word pierced Cushing like a blade, deep and hard and repellent. He knew people used it, increasingly, but he hated such foul language. But now he had the measure of the man, and the difference between them, and it gaped wide. In the full glare of the hall light, scarlet sweater radiant, a bloody breast swimming in the older man's vision, Gledhill wiped his long, shiny slug-like lower lip. "But I don't like people making allegations against me, okay? When they're lies. Complete lies, all right? What *normal* man would?"

Les loves that boy.

The low burr on the telephone line changed to a single long tone and Cushing tapped the cradle to get a line.

"Please go. Immediately, please. I don't want to continue this conversation."

"Mate, honestly..."

"I'm not your 'mate', Mr Gledhill, quite frankly."

His heart thudding in his ears, Cushing dialled with a forefinger he prayed was steady. The wheel turned anticlockwise with the return mechanism, waiting for the second '9'.

The cold had infiltrated and he felt it on his blue-lined skin as he stared at the long-haired man framed in his front doorway against the February night and the other did the same in return. Neither man dared give his adversary the satisfaction of breaking eye contact first. Gledhill hung onto the door frame, meaty hands left and right. Passingly, Cushing thought of Christopher Lee in his big coat as the creature in *Curse*. But all that monstrousness on the outside, for all to see.

He dialled a second time, straight-backed, not wanting to show the stranger he was afraid, but he *was* afraid. Of course he was afraid. He wasn't a young, athletic man any more, sword-fencing beside Louis Hayward or leaping across tables. Far from it. If this man chose to, cocky, powerful and threatened, he could stride right in and beat him to a pulp, or worse. There was no guarantee that a man prone to other acts, *despicable* acts, would be pacified by a threat of recrimination at a later date. Or a mere *phone call*. Criminals did not think of consequences. That was one of the things that defined them as criminals. There was nothing, literally nothing, to stop his unwelcome guest killing him, if he decided to.

For the third time he placed his index finger in the hole next to the number '9' and took it round the circumference of the dial.

"All right," Gledhill said. "All right. I'll say this, then I'm going. There's nothing going on here, okay? It's as simple as that. Nothing for you to be involved in. *Nothing*. Okay?"

Emergency. Which service do you require?

Cushing stared. Gledhill stared back.

Emergency. Hello?

Gledhill laughed with a combination of utter sadness and utter contempt. "Jesus Christ. You're as loopy as he is. You're losing your *fucking* marbles, old man."

Hello?

Then Gledhill left, slamming the door after him and the hall shook, or seemed to shake, like the walls of a rickety set at Bray, and Cushing did not blink and did not breathe until he was gone, and his after-image—the halo of redness—departed with him. Cut!

Hello?

"I'm most awfully sorry," he whispered into the receiver. "I thought I had an intruder. I can see now that's not the case." He tried to cover the tremor he knew was in his voice, and tried to make it light and chirpy. "I'm perfectly safe. Thank you."

Cushing hung up, re-knotted the cord of his dressing gown, hurried into the sitting room and parted the drawn curtains with his fingers, a few inches only, to see—nobody. Even the last fragment of light and colour had faded from the sky. It was now uniformly black and devoid of stars.

The dryness in Cushing's throat gave him the sudden compulsion to breathe, which he thought a very good idea indeed but strangely an effort. It was as if he had done a ten mile run, or heavy swim. Not only was his chest still thumping like a kettledrum, he could not get air into his lungs fast enough, and lurched, quite light-headedly, needing to prop himself on the arm of a chair in case he should fall. Sweat broke on his brow. He undid the buttons at his throat but they were already undone. He opened more, but his fingers were frozen and useless, fumbling and befuddled and half-dead.

This man who makes horrible, sadistic films about cruelty and sex and torture...

Someone who's never had any children of his own, they tell me... Someone who adores *other peoples' children...*

This old man and this innocent little boy...

Liquid surging up his gullet, he gagged and stumbled from the room to the little lavatory under the stairs, pressing his handkerchief to his mouth, but gagging nonetheless.

***

After he had vomited on and off for half an hour he half-sat, half-lay in the dark, drained and pathetic, too weak to move. What was the point of moving? He was clean here. He was untouched, though his fingers tingled from the bleach he had thrown liberally down the pan and the acid of it almost made him retch all over again. At least here, huddled on the cold linoleum, he could imagine the Domestos coursing through his veins, ridding him of the foul accusation that had contaminated his home. Here he could bury himself away from vile possibilities, horrid dangers, unspeakable acts and, yes, responsibility to others. What did others *want* of him anyway? He despaired.

What did his *conscience* want of him? To go to the police— with what? The fantasy of a backward child? A child with a vivid imagination, or psychiatric problems, or both? And what would that do but cause trouble, of the most horrifying nature, not least for himself? *An old man talking to a young boy*, he'd been accused of being by the boyfriend. The insinuation turned his stomach anew. What was wrong with that? How dare people misinterpret—but misinterpret they would: they *wanted* to misinterpret, that was the vile thing. Then again, what if he *himself* was misinterpreting? He could see it now, in a flash-forward, a dissolve: "Famous actor unhinged by grief." If he stepped forward and spoke up, *he'd* be just as likely the one arrested. Sent to prison. Shamed. *His* picture all over the newspapers. If he was pathetic now, how much *more* pathetic would he be behind bars, or even in the witness box? But what churned in his belly more than all of that was the terrible thought that his failure to act would suit the true offender down to the ground. The creature would be free to continue his cynical, sordid depredations to his heart's content. And that poor boy...

God...

He shut his eyes. He felt like the terrified Fordyce, the bank manager he played in *Cash on Demand*. Mopping perspiration from his brow. Prissy, emasculated, threatened. Affronted by the taunts of his nemesis. Goaded. His psychological flaws exposed. But that didn't help. What could he *do*? He wanted, wanted so desperately for someone to tell him. But who was there?

Aching and chilled, he clawed himself to his feet, clambered to the kitchen, poured himself lukewarm water from the tap, and drank. He needed Helen, his bedrock. Now more than ever.

He realised he felt so weak and ineffectual, not just now, but always. He remembered the spectacle of breaking down in tears in front of Laurence Olivier, thinking then, as he thought now: Am I strong enough? Am I strong enough for this?

Yes you are, Helen had reassured him. *If you want to be. You're worth ten of them, Peter. You're strong enough for anything...*

Back then, she'd nursed him through a nervous breakdown that had lasted a good six months. Dear Heaven, is that something this odious man could use against him now? His doctor's records of psychological unbalance? He felt the terrifying possibility like another blow to his physical being. The awful likelihood of the dim past regurgitated, raked over in mere spite and venom. It would bring with it dark clouds, as it had done then.

Six months of misery it had been, for him and for Helen too, without a doubt. God only knew how she'd endured it, but she had. And he had endured it too, thanks to her, and her alone.

How could it be, he'd wondered, that he, the husband, was supposed to protect her, and there she was, sacrificing everything completely selflessly so that he, this worthless actor, of all things, could pull through?

Then he could hear her voice again, even clearer this time:

Peter, you are completely unaware of your own value. I expect that's why I love you, and so do so many of your friends and colleagues. Can you not see? You must think more of yourself, darling, as we do. You do not need the backbiting and jealousy of the court of King Olivier. Your heart is not suited to it, and I know your enormous talent will out... You just need the right opportunity to come along, and it will... You must believe that too...

Once again he remembered her love and sweetness and once again he felt devastated. He teetered to the living room and collapsed in a chair.

Through the doorway to the hall he could see the pile of unread scripts and it reminded him of the single day of shooting at Elstree, just over a month earlier, on *Blood from the Mummy's Tomb*, the eleventh of January, the day he'd had the phone call to tell him Helen had been rushed to Kent and Canterbury Hospital. His scenes had been hurriedly rescheduled but Helen had died of emphysema at home on the Thursday. There was no question of him returning to the production. The already-filmed scenes with Valerie Leon were scrapped and the role written for him, that of the Egyptologist Professor Fuchs, given to Andrew Keir. Quatermass replacing Van Helsing. The curse of an ancient civilisation: it seemed like ancient history now.

Yet clear as a bell was his memory of wandering out alone, all, all alone onto the deserted beach just after Helen had breathed her last from those accursed lungs of hers, the seagulls reeling and swooping and cackling, the gale force wind hard in his face, the waves that crashed on the shingle sounding to him like a ghastly knell, the thoughtless pulse of the planet. And he'd sung *Twinkle, Twinkle Little Star*. He thought he'd gone a little mad that night.

Up above the world so high
Like a diamond in the sky...

He'd then found himself, unaware of the passage of intervening time, back at 3 Seaway Cottages, running up and down the stairs repetitively, endlessly, far beyond the point of exhaustion. To an impartial observer this might have given the appearance of madness too, but was anything but. In those moments he'd known exactly what he was doing. He'd ran up, ran down, ran up again and so on in the vain hope of inducing a heart attack so that he might be reunited with her. He may have cursed God too, a little, that night under the stars. God didn't approve of taking one's own life, but damn God. He'd wanted to be with Helen and that was all he cared about. Then, racing up and down, up and down, he stopped dead as he realised the cruelty of it all. That, if he did commit suicide, he might find himself in purgatory, or in limbo, and separated from Helen forever. The crushing realisation had hit him that *that* Hell would be even more unbearable than this, and he crumbled finally, spent.

Helpless, he'd found himself sitting on the stairs gasping for air, wheezing as she had wheezed, his lungs filling like bellows as he wept.

When the blazing sun is gone,
When there's nothing he shines upon,
Then you show your little light,
Twinkle, twinkle, through the night...

But God, as they say, moves in mysterious ways. And soon afterwards he had found the letter. Heard her voice as he'd read it:

"My Dear Beloved. My life has been the happiest one imaginable... Remember we will meet again when the time is right. Of that I have no doubt whatsoever. But promise me you will not pine... or, most of all, do not be hasty to leave this world..."

He had shivered then at the terrible thought that he might have, stupidly, done something so contrary to her wishes. Helen wanted him to go on, and he would go on. He would do what she wanted. He would do anything for her.

Do not be hasty to leave this world...

That's what she'd said to him. But the truth is, he thought, I didn't have the courage then, and I don't have it now.

Dear Peter, of course you do. Dying isn't hard. Living without the love of your life is hard. That's the hardest thing of all.

But now I am feeling more lost than ever...   the child, the boy...

You care. That is your greatest strength. People feel it. They see it on the screen.

But this isn't the screen. This is life.

You will know what to do. You make the right choices, Peter. Just believe in yourself. As I do, my darling. Always...

He remembered, as if being in the audience watching a scene on stage in a drawing-room play, his father telling him, without any note of malice or cruelty, as if it were a statement of fact like the earth revolving round the sun, that he, Peter, was forty and a failure.

Even the memory of the hurt made him take a quick, sharp breath. But he remembered also the way Helen had stood up to the old man and given him a piece of her mind. His father had never been talked to like that, and certainly not by a woman. The fellow hardly knew what had hit him. And afterwards, when the two of them were alone, what had she said to him?

You have to believe in yourself, Peter... Believe in yourself and your abilities and not be brought down by those lesser mortals who for some reason of their own want you not to succeed. God gave you an amazing gift, darling, and God wants it to soar, and so do I. Have faith in your talent. That's all you need, Peter... Faith, and love...

The stink of bleach burned in his nostrils. It clung to the air and he knew he would not be able to rid the house of it for days. Perversely, he inhaled it deeply, as an act of defiance, determined to breathe in his own house, undaunted.

Faith and love *were* all he needed. Faith in himself, and the love of Helen, which he knew was immortal. That would be enough to get him through. Even this turmoil. Even this pestilence. He suddenly knew it. He was not weak. He was not pathetic.

With her courage, he could soar.

***

The floor of the interview room was concrete under his feet, the walls whitewashed, the single window set with bars beyond the glass. An old window. A window with tales to tell. *If walls had ears*, the saying goes. Indeed so, he thought. He wondered if it had once been an actual cell and how often names, jibes, scrawls, remarks, obscenities had been eradicated with a new coat of paint. As possible lives had been eradicated, set on this path or that, turned, curtailed, saved, doomed, the guilty punished, the innocent punished come to that.

There was nothing on the table in front of him but his hands, so he stood and paced with them clasped behind his back. They were still dry and cold from the walk. The sea, so often heralded as life-giving, ossified them. Made them into a mummy's hands. Leather-like.

Old man...

He closed his eyes. Inside his skull images of the scene from the night before ran though his brain. Multiplied. He saw them again and again. Take after take. Wait a minute, in that one he's quite aggressive. That one, more sympathetic. The clapperboard snapped, making his eyes flicker. Close-up. Take eleven. Man steps from the shadows, his lips open in a horizontal grin... No, take twelve, smiling evilly, the hands rubbing together...

He always wondered how editors remembered every nuance, every glance or inflection: now, only twenty-four hours later, he had difficulty doing the same. Now he had trouble remembering if the man had said anything to incriminate himself—anything actual, *tangible*—or whether his threat and bluster was born out of sheer panic, a bombastic act of frightened self-defence. What did he know for certain? Just that Gledhill had verbally attacked only the person who'd verbally attacked *him* first, in his absence. Was that inhuman, the behaviour of a cornered animal? Or the all-too-human reaction of an innocent man?

You're losing your fucking *marbles, old man...*

He flinched again at the obscenity scrawled on his memory like graffiti on the wall of a public lavatory. Then saw Gledhill's face again, at the gap in the door.

An old man and a little boy...

The insidious words' capacity to appal him was undiminished, sickening him to his core. He took a deep breath and dispelled any misgivings. The man was a liar, and had shown his cards. Hadn't he?

Aware of a slump he normally only affected when 'old man acting' was required, he pushed his shoulders back, stretched his spine, scratched his chin, the bristles rasping there. While there was nothing on the walls to see himself in, in the mirror at home before setting out he'd seen a salt-and-pepper beard emerging, starting to give him a look like 'Dr Terror' from Milton's portmanteau extravaganza, though he knew the particular nastiness in this tale he was living was nothing so comfortably *outré* as ancestral werewolf, voodoo jazz or malignant vine. He wished to goodness it was. He wished he could even be as pragmatic and unflappable as his Inspector Quennell in *The Blood Beast Terror* when luring a gigantic moth to its inevitable flame. But it was all too easy to face monsters with a screenplay in your hand. Even a bad one.

The previous night he had slept in erratic bursts, but not as sporadically as the night before, and did not dream as he had feared he might after his encounter. The framed photograph of Helen had rested on the pillow at his side and the influence of too many third-hand superstitions from bad scripts made him feel it had fended off evil. He'd allowed the thought to comfort him without analysing it too much. Still sorely sleep-deprived, he had awoken at dawn spiky and brittle but strangely purposeful, and had played Berlioz's 'Royal Hunt' from *The Trojans* while he dressed, pausing only to turn it up louder. Twice.

The door opened, the turn of the handle surprisingly sibilant, and a thick-set man entered wearing a brown suit, beige shirt and mustard tie. The shirt had been acquired when he had less of a paunch, and consequently the buttons were under stress and had tugged the ends out above his belt. He ran his index fingers round the rim of his trousers to re-insert them before settling his rump in the chair at the table. His socks and some inches of bare, hairless leg were exposed above slip-ons.

"Peter."

"Derek, dear boy..."

"Did you get my card?" The man, in his thirties, had hair slicked back with Brylcreem, and his fluffy growth of incipient sideburns was both ginger and ill-advised.

"Yes." In fact, Cushing knew full well it was with all the other cards, in a pile on the bureau, unopened. He was an actor. He would act. "Thank you so much."

Inspector Derek Wake did not waste time.

"What can I do for you?"

His bluntness bordered on sounding like impatience. Whether the policeman was particularly busy or merely lacking in sensitivity, Cushing didn't want to consider. Perhaps neither man wanted to indulge in the ritual of feigned sympathy, feigned appreciation. Anyway it was unimportant. That was not why he was here.

He had been to the Inspector before for advice when preparing for a part. Usually he was greeted with a measure of perky, hand-rubbing delight, doubtless providing as it did a welcome diversion from the normal, irksome jobs officers of the law are tasked to perform, many of them unpleasant, many downright dangerous. Advising on a screenplay was many things, however 'dangerous' was not one of them. But today Wake was taciturn. Perhaps he had too many things of greater importance on his plate. Cushing didn't imagine meeting a man recently bereaved would make a seasoned copper awkward or restless, given his profession, but perhaps it did. Perhaps this is how he showed it.

He'd brought a few pages of script from *Scream and Scream Again*, the Christopher Wicking draft. He was taking a gamble that Wake hadn't seen the film and didn't know it had already been made and released a year ago.   He'd torn off the title page and said the film was called *Monster City*—not a bad title, he thought: he'd been in worse. His role had been Benedek, a Nazi-like cameo with only a couple of scenes, but he told Wake he was lined up to play the Alfred Marks part, Superintendent Bellaver, the Scotland Yard detective given the run around by a spate of vampiric serial murders.

For a full three-quarters of an hour he asked the policeman questions about playing Bellaver. How would he address his assistants? How would he talk to a murder suspect? Whether a line seemed plausible. Whether another was properly researched. And when Wake replied, he scribbled notes copiously in the margins, underlining or circling the text, *double-underlining* on occasion, when he received details of special, usable significance. This, he knew, would please Wake as a kind of flattery. These days people's hearts were warmed by an affiliation to Hollywood in the way that past generations were by touching the hem of royalty. But, of course it was all nonsense. He wasn't the slightest bit interested in the Inspector's advice, and was hardly listening to his answers. The important questions—the *vital* questions—were yet to come. He was treading water, if the man but knew it. He had a plan. And it was nothing to do with the neatly-formatted pages in front of him.

"Well, thank you. You've been most helpful. I shan't take any more of your time." Cushing rose from the chair. "I'm sure you have better things to do than talk to me." He shook hands in his sincere, country-parsonish way, buttoned up his coat and moved to the door. Whereupon he paused, his fingers fluttering next to his mouth—perhaps too theatrical a gesture?—before turning turned back to the seated detective.

"Yes?"

"Actually there's another script. Not a script, a story treatment I've been sent by a film company. Very intense. Very troubling. I'm not at all sure I shall accept the part, but..." He hesitated, tugged his lower lip, waved his hand as if dismissing the idea, criss-crossing his scarf on his chest, showing Wake his back then peeking back over his shoulder. "I feel in my bones the writer hasn't really done his homework. In a legal sense."

"Well, here I am. Run it by me. I'll be able to tell you if it rings true. In a police sense, at least."

"Are you sure? I don't like to—"

"Not at all. I enjoy it. You know I do. It livens up my tea break. Fire away."

"Very well." He sat back down and placed his fingertips together in a steeple. Very Sherlock Holmes. Too Sherlock Holmes? "This is a Canadian production. The lead is a Canadian actress who plays the mother. But they might film it in this country." He didn't like improvising, but in this instance an off-the-cuff quality was essential. The telling details were most important in a barefaced lie. "I play a headmaster. I suppose it's essentially a version of *M*." No flash of recognition. "The Fritz Lang film?" Still nothing. "The Peter Lorre movie? Set in Germany?"

"Oh."

"Have you seen it?"

"Yes, of course." Clearly he hadn't. "Remind me what it was about again."

"Lorre plays a disturbed man. A man who kidnaps and murders children. A child molester who becomes hunted down by society. A horrible character, paradoxically portrayed as sad and lonely and even strangely sympathetic."

"No, I've never seen it." The policeman stood up. "Why would anyone want to see a film about that?"

"These things happen in the world, I suppose."

"All the more reason not to put them in films. I go to the pictures to enjoy myself, I don't know about you." He stood, running his fingers round the rim of his belt yet again. "What did you want to ask me?"

"My, er, character has evidence against the, um, perpetrator..." His confidence had wavered. He speeded up his delivery. "In the story, I mean. Incriminating evidence. This is the crux of the plot. Evidence against a family member, not the vagrant who has already been arrested. And I'm curious. What would be the correct police procedure in a case like this?"

Wake shrugged, and having arranged his shirt and trousers to his temporary satisfaction, adjusted the knot of his tie. "We'd have to investigate. Long process. Doctors' reports. Court. It's complex. You'll have to give me the exact details and..."

"Everyone would be interrogated."

"Questioned. Yes. Obviously."

"And the boy?"

Another shrug. "Taken into care, straight off, any sniff of evidence. Whoosh. Can't take the risk. Get him out of there." The lick of a lighter on a cigarette tip. Secreted back in the jacket pocket. Smoke directed at the ceiling. "Mum and dad can squabble till the cows come home. Right little cheerful movie this is going to be. Not a comedy, I take it."

"No."

"No. Too right." With his hands on his hips now, the belly jutted unabashed. "Nobody does well out of these cases, I can tell you. Nobody goes home smiling, put it like that. Families get broken up, pieced together again. Except you can't piece them together again, can you? Worst of it is, unless you virtually catch the bloke red handed, it's one person's word against another, and often as not even the kid won't speak up against their own parent, even if they half kill them on a daily basis. And the mum sticks up for the feller like he's a bloody angel. So they get off scot free. Buggered up it is, really buggered up. To be honest, I hate it, more than anything." More smoke, through teeth this time. Breath of a quietly-seething dragon. "Sooner string them up and have done with it, ask me. Know the bloody liberals say, what if there's a miscarriage of justice? I say, tell you what. Cut their bloody balls off they won't do it again. I guarantee that."

Which was as much as Cushing needed to hear. He stood up and shook the man's hand generously in both of his.

"Thank you so much."

"Don't do it." The detective flicked ash into a metallic waste paper bin. "You don't want to be associated with that kind of rubbish."

"Perhaps not." One side of his mouth twitched. "I'll consider my various options. Definitely. Thank you, Derek."

Out in the corridor with the sound of a clattering typewriter nearby and garrulous laughter slightly more distant and out of sight, the old man heard from behind him:

"Peter, do you mind if we have a quick word? On an unrelated matter?"

It felt like a cold hand on his shoulder, which was absurd. Two uniformed constables passed him, a man and a woman. They both smiled, as if they recognised him. He touched the rim of his hat.

Smiling, he turned to see Wake leaning against the jamb of the doorway to the interview room, not smiling at all. The policeman switched off the light, closed the door and walked past him up the corridor in the direction of the sergeant's desk, then turned into a glass-sided office and sat behind a desk with several bulging manila files on it which he arranged in piles of roughly equal height.

When Cushing had stepped reluctantly into his office he stood up again, flattened his tie against his shirt front with the palm of his hand, and crossed the room to shut the door after him. The conversation and clacking of the typewriter became substantially quieter. Wake returned to his swivel chair.

"A man came in this morning and made a complaint about you."

"Oh?" He told himself not to betray anything in his expression. Certainly not shock, though that was what he was feeling. Now the reason for Wake's mood was all too clear. "May I ask who?"

"I'm not at liberty to say. I told him I'd prefer not to, but if he wanted to make it official, I'd make it official. But he was reluctant."

"I'll bet he was." Under his breath.

Had he heard? Wake's buttons really were straining across his midriff. "He was doing you a favour. He doesn't want to cause any trouble."

"What exactly did he say, Derek? Are you allowed to tell me that? Officially or unofficially?"

"He said you were talking to his little boy."

"That's absolutely correct. I was. I won't deny that. What's wrong with that?"

"Let's just say he doesn't want it." The way he lounged back in the chair was beginning to annoy Cushing. He found it louche, oikish and disrespectful. And the man's fly zip was distressingly taut.

"I chat to all the children. You know that. They chat to me. I'm like the Pied Piper. Helen and I..."

"I know. I know." Wake leant forward, elbows on the desk. Pushed the harshness of the angle-poise lamp away. "Listen, it puts me in a very awkward position. When someone comes in with a complaint like this. I don't want it to go any further if I can help it."

"On my part?"

"On anybody's part."

Cushing could feel his lips tight and bloodless with rage and dared not speak for fear of what might come out. So, he's got his retaliation in first, he was thinking. Clever. Before I could make any accusations, he's made his.

Clever man.

Clever monster.

"Look, I know this feller. He's a hell of a nice bloke." Wake raked his hair with his fingers and offered his palms. "We went to school together. I've got drunk with him. He's not a troublemaker, not like some round here. He's got a decent job, down on the boats. My wife knows his family, has done for donkey's years. He visits his mum in the nursing home every Sunday. He helps out at Christmas, with the food and that."

"In other words, you believe him."

"I think things can be misinterpreted, that's all," Wake said. "And he has, probably. I don't mean 'probably'."

Cushing didn't think he could remember such anger building up inside him. It was white hot and it terrified him and he knew if it rose much more he wouldn't be able to control it, and that would be a disaster. He opened the door.

"Thank you so much. I think I'll go now, if you don't mind. Unless you have anything more to say to me."

Wake sighed and rubbed his eyes.

When he looked up to reply, Cushing was gone. Wake sprang up, grabbed the closing door of his office, yanked it back wide and hurried to the sergeant's desk in pursuit of the long dark coat. Remarkably, the older man was out-striding him and he had to break into a run to catch up.

"Peter. Let me drive you home."

"No, Derek. Thank you all the same. I think I'd prefer some nice fresh sea air. Good day to you."

The detective followed him outside, caught up with him a second time and stood in front of him on the pavement, this time blocking his way.

"Look, all I'm suggesting to both of you is keep a wide berth from each other. You, and Gledhill and his family. Both parties.

Either that, or sort out your differences without the police getting involved."

"I'm sure we shall," Cushing said, circumnavigating him.

***

The scenario had changed radically. The script had been rewritten, drastically. Now at least he knew with some certainty that he daren't rely on the police or the legal system. His adversary had prepared the ground, cleverly sown the seeds of doubt in a pre-emptive strike against him. If he made an accusation now it was too risky he would be disbelieved and, worse, far worse, the *boy* would be disbelieved—if the boy even spoke up at all. There was no guarantee he would do so, given his only way of dealing with the situation, it seemed, was through the prism of monsters and monster-hunters. Wasn't it Van Helsing who said "The Devil's best trick is that people don't believe he exists"? In Bram Stoker's novel, he thought, but certainly in the play and Universal film. He remembered the Van Helsing of the book: a little old man who literally talked double Dutch. He remembered asking Jimmy Carreras why he didn't cast a double-Dutchman in the part, and Jimmy saying: "We rather think you should play him as yourself". But the point was, how should he play *this* part, now? He had to stop this man. Alone, if need be. And he needed ammunition. In the words of Inspector Wake, he needed *evidence*.

Without delay he resolved to visit the Fount of All Knowledge.

She was wrapping up a cucumber in newspaper for a customer with whom she was conversing breathlessly. Through a steady stream of clients like this one she gleaned her vital information. A round-faced woman with the general shape of the Willendorf Venus and the given name of Betty, she knew everything to know about everyone in town: even a good deal they didn't know about themselves, he suspected. When Helen and he came to buy fresh vegetables from her and her husband's shop, they invariably came away a little wiser about something of high import, locally. In the woman's opinion, anyway. Which is why Helen had coined her nickname: 'The Fount of All Knowledge', and it had stuck. A private joke between Peter and his wife. A private look between them as she twirled a bag of tomatoes at the corners whilst dispensing the latest gossip. A private raised eyebrow. A private hand concealing a wry smile. It seemed so long ago, and only yesterday.

"Lovely morning."

"Hello, Mr C. Yes it is." She wiped the dry earth from her hands to her apron. "The sun's done us proud. For February."

"I should like one of these, please."

The Fount of All Knowledge took the cabbage from his hands and popped it into a brown paper bag tugged from a butcher's hook. The tiny stigma in the corner torn.

"Good to see you out, sir." She looked down at her shuffling feet. "We know how it must be for you. Everyone's been saying."

"Bless you."

"Everybody knows how much you loved each other. I'm sure that's no comfort to you at all." Her cheeks reddened appreciably. "Still..."

He held out a handful of coins—the new decimal currency, still a struggle—and allowed her to take the required amount. "I am comforted by the certainty that I will be united with her one day. Of that I have no doubt whatsoever." He smiled. The woman nodded to herself, then rang up the money in a till secluded in the shadows under the awning. "Tell me, my dear. You may be able to help me. Do you by any chance know a woman by the name of Mrs Drinkwater? She has a boy named Carl."

"Annie?"

"Possibly. She lives in a bungalow on Rayham Road."

"That's the one." She picked up a broom and started brushing between the stalls. "Her brother had a hole in the heart. You know, like that footballer."

Cushing nodded but had no idea what she was talking about.

"I wonder, do you know whether she still takes in ironing? I believe her circumstances may have changed recently. I don't want to cause offence by enquiring unnecessarily. Someone tells me she has a new young chap in her life."

The Fount of All Knowledge shook the box of potatoes. "For all the good it'll do her."

"Oh? You sound sceptical."

"I wonder why."

"I've heard nothing but good reports of him. Les, I think his name is. He's excellent with the boy, apparently. Perhaps I've heard wrongly."

"Not got a great track record, has he? Married before. Divorced."

"We don't condemn people for that, do we? Not these days."

"I don't condemn anybody for anything, me." She took a large handful of carrots from a new customer. "I don't repeat what's told to me in confidence. I just wouldn't trust him as far as I could throw that building over there."

This was exactly the kind of information he wanted. But he wanted more. "His first wife? Now, was that Valerie Rodgers, the hairdresser from The Boutique, by any chance?"

"No. Nice girl from Tankerton. Sue something. Blezard, as was. That's it. Works in a tea shop in Canterbury. Pilgrims, I think it's called."

That was all he wanted to know, and the rest of the conversation consisted in a short discussion of who might take in his ironing. He weathered that particular storm until the Fount of All Knowledge ran out of intellectual steam, for which he was abundantly grateful. He touched the rim of his hat. *Bless you. Goodbye.* Which is when *Mr* Fount of All Knowledge appeared from the back of the shop holding aloft a pleat of garlic in two hands, eager to share the joke as if it were the first time he'd thought of it—which it most surely wasn't.

"Garlic, Mr C?"

"Very droll, Mr H," Peter Cushing said, as he always did. "Very droll."

***

He ran for the bus fearing he'd miss it, and by the time he settled into a seat his lungs were on fire. The pain and breathlessness reminded him of Helen's lungs as the vehicle pulled away from the bus station.

Sadly he realised that he had always kept working to provide for their future together. An old age together without financial worries that was not to be. It made him feel foolish, not that he could have known it would happen like this—never *like this*—but somehow feeling God, a force for good, unaccountably laughed at one's futile plans. Still, the income he had provided from films was able to give Helen a few luxuries, as well as the all-important medical care and attention when her cough got worse and her breathing painful and difficult. He remembered the arrival of the oxygen mask and canister necessary to assist her lungs. Meanwhile he, as Frankenstein, effortlessly transplanted brains and brought back the dead.

Frankenstein always failed because his morality was flawed, because his drive to help humanity was misguided. But in reality doctors failed for much more mundane reasons. When they went to Dr Galewski, the pulmonary specialist, he'd said: "You have

left it too late. You should have come to me ten years ago."
Frankenstein had never uttered a line so heartless.

He'd taken Helen to France, driving his spanking new blue
Mark IX Jaguar to the thermal springs at Le Mont-Dore, spending
hours on meditative walks in the hills while his wife rested.
Encountering solitary goatherds as he grew a moustache for his
next role. Telling her his silly adventures every evening. He
remembered how, day by day, her laughter had grown stronger.
How she was revitalized by the experience. The doctor from
Poland had performed a minor miracle after all. Her cough had
disappeared.

But the precious respite was to be hideously short-lived. Her
throaty laughter cut short.

The Return of the Cybernauts in *The Avengers*; *Corruption*;
The Blood Beast Terror...

All as her illness worsened.

They decided to sell Hillsleigh, their place in Kensington—
Helen had said London "smelled of stale food and smoke"—and
move permanently to their beloved holiday home by the sea. He
remembered the pitiful sight of her sitting at the bottom of the
stairs saying, "Can we go there, please?"

"Of course, my love. Of course."

He had kissed her and held her in his arms. He'd always joked
in interviews that they'd married for money: he had £15 and she
had seventeen and ten. That came back to him now.

He thought mostly of all the wasted time travelling back and
forth to London when he could have been at her side. Fifteen
televised hours of the horrid, under-rehearsed BBC *Sherlock
Holmes*, an experience he loathed, distracted as he was by Helen's
condition, barely able to remember his lines. He remembered the
stair lift being installed in 3 Seaway Cottages whilst he was
shooting *Frankenstein Must Be Destroyed*—"Hammer's Olivier,

impeccably seedy in his spats and raspberry smoking jacket," the New York Times said of him in that one. He remembered her reading it aloud to him, delighting in the phrase as she repeated it. And Amicus's Jekyll and Hyde variation *I, Monster*, catching the milk train to filming because he couldn't bear to spend so much as a night away from her.

After a short, callous period when she'd seemed to recuperate, Helen's respiration had become laboured again. He'd employed dear Maisie Olive to help with the housework because his wife was unable to function any more as the wife she wanted to be. That cut him to the quick, when she'd said it with tears in her eyes. But he didn't want a wife. He wanted *her*.

Her spirits lifted slightly as she decided almost on a whim that breathing exercises were the answer. He'd been buoyed by her sudden optimism but just as quickly her hopes were dashed by a young locum who told her they were a waste of time. He had wanted to strangle the man there and then, just like one of his villains would have done. He'd done it endless times on screen: how difficult could it be in real life? Or take one of those hacksaws of Baron Frankenstein and cut round his skull like a boiled egg, as he did to poor Freddie Jones. Take out that thoughtless brain of his. But the truth was, nothing he could do or think or dream would make the slightest difference to Helen's future, as well he knew.

As it was, that slap in the face by the locum took the heart out of her. He saw it. At that point exactly her spirit crumbled. And he feared his would too, but he dare not let it. He dreaded that her seeing an inner agony written in his features would compound her own. He would act. Act. Act. Act.

He gazed out of the filthy window of the bus. The countryside lay under a gauze of grime and dead insects.

On December the sixteenth, he had his last job before Helen died. Recording *The Morecambe and Wise Special* for transmission on the coming Christmas Day. As scripted, he was required to appear unexpectedly beside Eric and Ernie to complain he hadn't been paid the five pounds for an earlier show. It was a running gag: quite a good one, he thought. People had enjoyed his "corpsing" when he had guest-starred for the first time playing King Arthur, and it was gratifying that the team had asked him back. Helen had said, go on, it would do him good to play against type. To show there was a side of him that was warm and humorous and bright. The side she knew and loved.

Bring me sunshine...

He had thought he could get through it, and he had. Now, once again, he could hear the audience laughing through the grime and gauze of the world around him.

Bring me sunshine...

Even then, he had known deep down that, while the nation roared with laughter, his wife was at home, dying.

***

"Cream tea for two, please." He said it automatically, without thinking. "No, how stupid of me." He smiled. "I mean a pot of tea for one, and a single scone with jam and clotted cream. If you'd be so very kind." He placed the plastic menu back behind the tomato sauce bottle. "Thank you, my dear."

"Thank you." She finished scribbling on her little pad using a Biro with a feather Sellotaped to it in order to resemble a quill pen.

"Excuse me. I'm terribly sorry. Sue?"

"Yes?"

It hadn't been hard to find The Pilgrim Tea Room on Burgate after a short meander through Canterbury's narrow streets. It couldn't have looked more like a tea room if it had tried, with its dark timbers and white-painted plasterwork overhanging a bulging bow window. If not Elizabethan it had a distinctly

Dickensian feel about it. He could imagine Scrooge walking by, muffled against the cold in a heavy snowfall, wishing everybody a Merry Christmas and carol singers holding lanterns on sticks. Not a bad role, Scrooge. He would have made a decent fist of it, he thought, had it ever been offered.   Standing outside the restaurant, it struck him The Pilgrim was exactly the kind of emporium he and Helen would have gravitated to on one of their day trips. Exactly the kind of place Helen would have chosen. He had almost felt her arm tighten around his, guiding him in.

"Do you mind if I have a quick word? Whilst it's not too busy. I don't want to interrupt your work. It'll only take a moment, I promise."

The woman looked confused and a little frightened. As well she might be. He didn't blame her.

"We're about to close."

"It won't take long, I promise."

She hesitated. "I'll put this order in first, if you don't mind."

"No, of course, my dear. Please do."

He watched her glide to the far end of the shop, collecting empty plates and cups on the way. A Kentish Kim Novak dressed in a black ankle-length dress with a pinny over it, her hair pinned up under a frilly bonnet, the sort Victorian kitchen maids used to wear. It was an illusion dissipated somewhat by white plimsolls that had seen better days, and the lipstick. The overall effect was cheap and, combined with the ridiculously Heath Robinson quill, somewhat absurd. But the whole place was grubbily inauthentic, designed to milk the tourists for a quick bob or two. History was merely its gimmick. She returned with a damp cloth in her hand and wiped down the plastic table cloth. He lifted his elbows to give her room for her comprehensive sweeps and lunges.

"I've seen your films." She lifted the duo of sauce bottles out of the way one by one. "You're Christopher Lee aren't you?"

He corrected her with consummate politeness, tugging on his white cotton glove.

"No, I'm the other one."

"Vincent Price?"

He kept his smile to himself. "That's right."

He pulled the ash tray towards him and lit one of his cigarettes.

"I'd like to talk to you about Les Gledhill."

The sweeping actions of her arm were energetic but he detected the tremor of a pause which she quickly attempted to hide. The skin on her face seemed to tighten, betraying a tense irritation. Her former relaxed, if busy, manner was suddenly gone. It was as if he had flipped a switch in one of his Frankenstein laboratories and she suddenly looked ten years older.

"You know what? I don't want to know about him. I don't want anything to do with him. He's a nasty piece of work. A sick, nasty piece of work." The swirling motions of the damp cloth on the table became violent, as well as repetitive.

"Did you know he's with another woman now?"

"I hope they'll be very happy together."

"She has a boy."

The woman stopped wiping the table top within an inch of its life and stood up straight. He saw her hand tighten round the dish cloth which she had swapped from one hand to the other. Her knuckles whitened and a few drops of water exuded, hanging like tiny baubles from the joints of her fingers.

"Look, I don't know why you're interested in him and I don't want to know. I don't even want to remember his name. But I have remembered it, thanks to you."

She turned away but he shifted quickly onto the nearer chair and caught her hand. The one with the damp rag. He felt its wetness seeping through her fingers to his.

"The boy is called Carl. I'm concerned about him, and I'm concerned about his mother." He was looking up into her face but her eyes were darting around the room now, afraid that the scene was drawing attention.

"Please. I don't want this man to ruin any more lives. I want to stop him. Is there anything you can tell me? Anything?"

She looked down into the blueness of his eyes. She pulled away her hand, abruptly, to her side, holding it there, then seemed to realise it was an unkindness that was unnecessary to an old man.

"I wish I knew then what I know now, that's all."

"Which is what? Please."

Her voice remained hard, terse with discomfort and something else swimming vast and unpleasant under the surface.

"He fastens onto vulnerable women. He can spot them. He homes in. He uses them. To get what he wants."

He knew she'd already said too much and regretted it. Horribly so. Giving the table a last, cursory wipe, she turned on her heel and walked towards the kitchen with her shoulders back, eyes front. A teenage boy with his head haloed in the fur-trimmed hood of a parka sat at one of the other tables with his shoes, laces undone, planted on a chair. She flicked his shoulder with the back of her hand as she passed by, hardly looking at him.

"Feet. Off."

The youth shot her a fierce look from under a heavy fringe. His mane of dark hair shook as he did so. His nose was long and square with a slight line above the tip from rubbing it too much. His eyebrows had begun to join in the middle. Thick lips, succulent yet dry enough to crack. Slightly crooked teeth. A constellation of pimples on his cheeks, some livid red, others turning yellow with pus. The affliction of the young. Another of God's little cruelties.

"Mum..." he complained in a sing-songy way under his breath.

Cushing felt an intense chill and imagined someone had opened and closed the door, but they hadn't.

He looked over at the boy in the parka as the latter played with the sugar dispenser, pouring a measured spoonful onto the table then scooping it, plough-like, with the flat of one hand then the other, prodding it into a perfect square, then making a dot in the centre of the square with the top of his index finger. Then destroying the whole artistic arrangement and starting again. He appeared both to be completely absorbed in the activity and completely bored by it. There was a lazy insouciance in the lad's countenance, something about his very physicality which bordered on barely-contained rage.

What had Van Helsing said in *Brides*? That he was studying a sickness. A sickness *part physical, part spiritual...*

As if aware of being spied on, the youth looked up. Their eyes met and he knew the old man was staring at him. His features froze, but not with any degree of guilt or foreboding. Without any fraction of self-consciousness or embarrassment. Quite the reverse. He stared back at Cushing with chilling assuredness. Aggression, in fact. A hard gaze, a vicious gaze which would take almost nothing to provoke to violence, and the old man wondered if he had provoked it already, and it scared him to the core to think of what a young man with such a cold gaze might be capable.

"I've said all I'm going to say to you."

It was Sue Blezard's voice again as she placed his cream tea on a tray in front of him.

"I understand."

"No. You don't," she said.

But he feared he did. Very much so.

"Always the one to take the boy to bed..." She stood with her back to her son, blocking him out. "Read him a story. Their 'special time', he said..." It was as if she didn't even realise she'd said the words. Her anger had said them, spilled them, from some disembodied place, before she'd had a chance to rein them back. Then her back stiffened. That was all. No more. The muscle in her cheek flexed. "Pay at the till when you're ready."

She walked away.

"Thank you," Cushing said, knowing that she had revealed more than she could bear and no less than she was compelled. He respected that. In seeking to end pain, he had caused it, and hated himself for doing so. But it was necessary. So necessary.

The cup and saucer were Wedgwood. He thought it pathetic that he cared about such things.

Some of the pustules on the lad's skin had broken and there were small streaks of blood where they had been picked at. After some minutes his mother brought the youth a hot chocolate and Cushing continued to watch him as he drank it. There were cuts and bruises on his hands as well as nicotine stains, and his fingernails were chewed to the quick. His knee jiggled with the spastic tremor of an old and hopeless alcoholic. It spoke of an inexorable slide into a life Cushing did not want to contemplate. Where was this boy? Not in school, clearly. Then, <u>where</u>?

He thought of hurt and anger... the road to dissolution, evil, decay.

Their special time...

The hurt that prowls.

The scar that infects.

The darkness that perpetuates itself.

He stirred his tea. When he drank it, it was cold.

***

Afterwards, for a stroll, he visited the Cathedral. It was only yards away and he had not set foot inside for years. He was surprised to find the interior so vast and daunting, more so than he ever remembered feeling before. A massive, overwhelming, empty space. A space in which you could fit several normal-sized cathedrals, certainly. He thought of it now, quite literally. Dozens and dozens of churches, stacked like Lego bricks. He wondered if there was any limit to how large the masons could build an edifice to proclaim their faith? How big does Faith have to be to fill a space the size of this? How much love does God need?

The last tourists of the day moved around the aisles, looking up in awe and wonder, but he was the only one who knelt in the pews and prayed.

With his eyes tightly closed, he heard a baby crying. The sound echoed distinctly in the Cathedral's canyon of stone, but when he stood and looked all round, he could see nobody. No baby. No mother. Nothing. And all was absolutely quiet again. Except for the side door creaking gently as it closed to keep out the sun.

***

He did not know how long he had been sitting in the bath but the water was stone cold and the Imperial Leather had turned it milky and opaque. He felt pins and needles in his bony buttocks so he thought he'd been there a long while, but it worried him he didn't know how long and now his shoulders were shivering and he was sure that under the scummy water his penis had shrunk to nothing. He wanted to pull the towel off the rail but it was slightly out of reach. Then the door of the bathroom opened and Christopher Lee came in, dressed exactly as he had been in the first Hammer *Dracula* in that formidable entrance descending the staircase. Immaculate hair. Virile. Vulpine. The top of his head almost touched the ceiling as he paced back and forth beside the claw-foot bath in his ankle-length black cloak. He looked terribly upset. "Where's my wife?" he was saying. "Where is she?"

Cushing could do nothing. He felt frozen and invisible.

He woke feeling the millstone presence of death, its crushing inevitability, in a way that he hadn't been so frightened by, or made helpless by, since he was seven years old.

Staring at the ceiling, he thought of the youth in the Pilgrim Tea Rooms, but instead of the pimply, hunched teenager in the parka, the boy sitting there was Carl Drinkwater, his hands wedged between his thighs, staring down at the plastic table-top which his mother was wiping with a wet cloth. Carl looked up and stared, just as the other boy had done. He had tiny smears of blood on his cheeks like the squashed bodies of dead insects.

***

Like massing vultures they gathered in the sky over the concourse of carrion, an echo of the prehistoric and primal. As the soles of his wellington boots pressed into the shingle with a hushing musicality of their own, their beckoning grew louder, a virulent and unforgiving choir. An announcement, spiteful heralds of his coming. Had he been blind, he thought, he could have purely followed the direction of the cries of the seagulls and found his way to the Harbour, where death was perpetually on the menu.

He carried a shopping basket. Not exactly becoming for a gentlemen, but he didn't care. It was his late wife's, and now it was his. He remembered the two *Harvesters* in the fifties, when he and Helen had first come here, often used as umpire boats during the regatta. The remains of the railway were still there, the lamp standards still in evidence though the tracks were gone. Two whelk boats still operated on East Quay, commercial ships came in carrying stone and timber, Danish stuff, he was told, and beyond West Quay he often saw grain boats unloading into lorries with a hopper.

Meanwhile fishing boats unloaded their silvery spoils and the gulls were there, hovering, fighting the wind, ready to clash and kill for the pickings they could get from what bloody morsels fell before the trucks loaded up and shipped it out. Old families tended to work the trawlers. Generations. Fathers, sons, grandfathers.

A sheen of blood and seawater striped the concrete. His wellingtons crossed the mirror of it in the direction of the ugly store shed on South Quay, corrugated asbestos on a breezeblock frame, both its barn doors open to the wide 'U' of the Harbour, the air punctuated by the tinkling of pulley metal and puttering slaps of wet ropes and lapping water.

It wasn't hard to find out the time of the tides and discover when exactly the boats came in, and he wasn't the only one who gravitated to the Harbour to get the pick of the 'stalker'—as they called the odds and sods, small fry not sorted with the prime fish already boxed up and ready on its way to London. If they were regulars, they'd know when a certain boat would berth and they'd be there waiting for the bargains when it returned on the flood tide.

He watched as fishermen in sou'westers and oilskins hurried up and down the ladder on and off the vessel. They weren't hanging around, even with a small crowd present. Business took precedence. A small truck waited, taking the stacked plastic boxes—the catch already sorted during the two-hour steam back from fishing off Margate in Queen's Channel—straight to market.

Les Gledhill was one of them, strands of long wet hair hanging from his hood, cheekbones shiny and doll-like over his damp beard. The stalker was bagged up and marked at the quayside beyond the parked cars, some of it wrapped in newspaper. No airs and graces. "5 Dover sole's £1." The misappropriated apostrophe was almost obligatory. Others who'd arrived first were helping themselves, and Gledhill was taking their cash in a wet, outstretched palm, skin peeled pink from the scouring weather.

Seeing Cushing out of the corner of his eye, Gledhill at first attempted to ignore him. A transistor radio set on an empty oil drum was playing the recent Christmas hit, 'Grandad' by Clive Dunn. Unable to avoid doing so any longer, Gledhill stared at him as he rinsed his hands under a cold water tap on the quayside and wiped them in a towel. The DJ on the radio switched to the current single at the top of the charts, George Harrison singing 'My Sweet Lord'.

"What do you have today?" Cushing presented himself as bright-eyed and bushy tailed.

"Depends what you're after."

"Oh, I think I'm open to suggestions." Cushing smiled broadly.

"Well. Got a load of dabs," Gledhill said, forcing a retaliatory smile to match. "Sprats. Herrings. Good winter fish. Dover sole. Skate. Nice skate backbone, if you know what to do with it." His hands looked frozen and painful to the older man as he watched him turn to serve an elderly woman who had the right change. A great deal of nattering was going on between the other customers and the other fisherman—quite sprightly, good-natured banter—and to an onlooker, this conversation would seem no different.

Cushing adjusted his scarf, scratched the side of his chin and pointed at one of the packages lined up before him. "That one will do perfectly."

"Pound."

"Thank you." Cushing happily delved into his purse.

Gledhill picked up the fish in newspaper and handed it to him, and as he did so Cushing saw the blue blur of an old tattoo on the back of his wrist, together with blue dots on his finger joints.

"You know, I was reading the other day..." He placed a pound note in the other man's palm. "The fish, it's the old symbol of Christianity. Older even than the cross."

"Fascinating," Gledhill said.

"Yes, it is, rather. Some people say religion has lost its way, but we are all God's children, when all is said and done. Whether we choose to see that or not. Don't you think?"

"You've got a bargain there, squire. I'd go home very happy if I were you."

Turning his back, Gledhill went back to the tap of ice cold water and washed his red raw hands with the thoroughness of a surgeon. Cushing had researched surgeon's methods for the Frankenstein films and it was the kind of thing he watched and made a mental note of, habitually. He found it interesting, vital, that there were telltale rituals and practices that made a profession look authentic, or inauthentic if wrong. It was essential to make the audience believe in the part one was playing, however ludicrous the part may be on paper. That was one's job. That was why they called it 'make believe'. Make. Believe.

Cushing waited.

Believe in yourself, Peter...

"Anything else you want, mate?" Gledhill turned his head and stared at the old man. "Apart from the Dover sole?"

Peter Cushing decided he would not be hurried. Why should he be?

"Let me see..."

He lingered. And the more he lingered the more he realised he was enjoying the discomfort his lingering engendered.

Les Gledhill did not do anything so obvious as a quick, shifty look towards his colleagues to reveal his unease. He would never have been that blatant. Nor did he become twitchy or self-conscious in any way. In fact his motions became slower and more considered. That, in itself, told a story—that the very presence of the old man in wellington boots made him uneasy. And he didn't like it. A person who got a certain thrill from the control of others seldom enjoyed the feeling that someone else had control of him.

"Have you ever tasted oysters, Mr Cushing?" Gledhill picked up one of the shelled creatures from a plastic bucket in front of him.

"I thought the oysters round here had all succumbed to disease and pollution."

"Not if you know where to look. I think of it as a hobby. Go out on a Sunday. Maybe get a hundred. You haven't answered my question. Sir." His intention was to intimidate, rather than *be* intimidated. That much was clear.

"My preference is towards plain food."

"Then you don't know what you're missing. Marvellous stuff." Gledhill took a knife from a leather satchel. It was a short, stubby one with a curve in the blade. "You break them open." Metal scraped against the shell. He turned the object in his hand and opened it as if it were hinged. "Dab of vinegar if you prefer. Or just as it comes." He ran the knife under the slimy-looking bivalve, cutting its sinewy attachment. It sat in its juices. "Then into the mouth they go." He slid it off the half-shell onto his tongue, savouring it for a second or two, no longer, then swallowed. "One bite. Two at the most. Then down like silk. Nectar. Nothing like it."

"Not for me."

"Not for everybody, that's for sure. Some people find it repulsive. Some can't even bear the idea and run a mile. But to gourmets, those who appreciate the good things in life, well... they're a little taste of Heaven." Gledhill's eye was steady again. Unblinking. "Acquired taste, of course..."

"If you say so."

"Don't knock it 'til you try it. As they say."

"Something eaten whilst it is still alive, simply in order to give a person pleasure? I find that rather... obscene."

"In a way. In another way, it's the peak of civilized behaviour. The stuff of banquets and kings. Of aristocracy and riches and palaces. The supreme indulgence. The Romans introduced them here two thousand years ago. Long ago as the time of Christ. Makes you think, doesn't it?"

"Perhaps."

"Lot of algae and low in salinity, the Thames Estuary. Knew a thing or two, those Romans." He tossed away the empty shell into a bucket half-full of them, shortly to add to the 'cultch' bed upon which the 'spat' of the next generation would settle. "Besides. If we humans don't live for pleasure, what do we live for?"

Cushing thought for a moment.

"Love?" he suggested. But really it was nothing like a question, to his mind.

Gledhill gave a snort, as if it were a bad joke, and wiped his hands in the grubby towel.

"Anything else I can do for you, sir? Or will that be all?"

"Actually there is one thing." Cushing was careful to maintain a matter-of-fact air. "I'm going to a matinee at the Oxford Picture House this afternoon. I rather thought you might like to join me."

Gledhill did not look away. "I don't like going to the cinema as a rule. Not in the daytime."

"Don't tell me you're afraid of the dark?" Cushing's wit fell upon deaf ears. "I'm sure you can make an exception."

"I'm busy."

"I think not. Your working day is evidently over."

"I didn't say I was working, I said I was busy."

"Oh. That's a shame." Cushing feigned disappointment. "It really is a shame. Because I've been to see your ex-wife and son, you see. Yes. Sue and I had a most edifying chat, and I thought you might be interested in what she had to say. It was quite—what can I say? Quite—special. I'm being dreadfully presumptuous. I shall go alone." He placed the wrapped Dover sole deep in his shopping basket and walked away a few steps before turning back, as if the next thing he said was a mere afterthought. "I believe the main feature commences at half past two. I do so hate missing the start of a picture, don't you? You can't really enjoy a story unless you see it from the beginning, right through to the bitter end. Don't you find?"

Gledhill was still staring at him. A few foolishly courageous seagulls descended in a flurry on the 'stalker' in front of him and took stabs at it, one trying to skewer some fish offal in rolled-up newspaper. Gledhill stamped his feet and clapped his hands, yelling sharply and waving his arms to scare them off. "Go! *Go!* Bloody pests!" Behind him, another fisherman directed a high-powered hose to wash down the flag stones. The gulls took to the skies.

Cushing tapped his shopping basket before walking away.

"Thank you for this. I shall enjoy it."

***

Fetching coal to build the fire for that coming evening, he remembered entering the same way from the garden, closing the door with his foot, finding Helen hunched on the divan looking like a frightened child. "I thought you'd left me." "I'm not going anywhere," he'd reassured her. She'd closed her eyes. He'd wrapped a blanket round her and made a fire, as he did now on his knees before the grate. He screwed up sheets of old newspaper in makeshift balls and laid a criss-cross pattern of kindling on top of them.

Maisie Olive had brought tea and said, "She'll be all right, sir."

He'd been smoking a cigarette. "Thank you, yes. She'll be all right."

At nine o'clock the night nurse helped Helen to bed. The last thing she said, clutching his hand, was, "Goodnight, Peter. God bless you."

At three o'clock some instinct he could not explain woke him, and he found her skin cold and clammy to his touch. He switched on the light and the electric blanket and went down to make tea. Her pupils were small dots. He fluffed up pillows and prised them behind her. When he returned with the tea, the night nurse was there saying her breathing was painful and then what breathing there was, painful or not, stopped.

The nurse looked at him and shook her head.

He looked down at Helen and saw all pain and suffering gone from her face. She was serene and at peace. The nurse must have seen his stricken features because she extended her arms, then lowered them.

At that moment Cushing had felt nothing, just a supreme hollowness inside. He'd thought, most strangely of all, if this was in a film I wouldn't be reacting like this at all. I'd be shouting and jumping around and wailing.

"You'd better get dressed now, Mr C," the night nurse said. He was still sitting in the armchair with the tea tray on his lap and it was daylight.

When the undertakers came, they showed him an impressively shiny catalogue of head stones. Many of them reminded him of the ones made out of polystyrene in the property shop at Bray. He'd been in a few graveyards in his time. Most of them taken apart afterwards to be reconstituted as other sets: barn, ballroom, bedroom. If only life could be dismantled, he thought, remade and reconstructed the way sets were, with a fresh lick of paint, good enough for the camera to be fooled. After looking at the brochure, he'd given the undertaker only one absolute specification for the gravestone: that there be a space left beside Helen's name for his own.

In that last year her weight had diminished drastically to under six stone, while he himself lost three. It was as if, unconsciously, he'd been keeping pace with her decline, wanting to go with her every step of the way—and beyond, if necessary.

The previous summer he had dropped out of filming Hammer's *To Love a Vampire*, the follow-up in the Sheridan Le Fanu 'Karnstein' saga (even though the part of occultist schoolmaster Giles Barton had been written for him) because Helen had become gravely ill, yet again.

"No more milk train," he'd said.

When she'd been rushed to hospital that last time and he'd been telephoned by Joyce at the studios, he was shocked how tired she looked when he arrived at her bedside. It was immediately clear this was not just a case of a few check-ups, as he'd deluded himself into thinking. He'd held her hand tightly and said to her he wasn't on call the next day and he'd bring in a picnic lunch. She smiled and said that'd be lovely. But when he'd arrived with the wicker hamper, like some character from a drawing-room farce, the nurses had told him he was not to be admitted under any circumstances. The doctors said his wife had had a serious relapse and her heart and lungs were terribly weak. He heard very little after that.

He succeeded by sheer persistence in persuading the specialists to let her home. Nobody precisely said that these coming days were her last, but their acquiescence made it obvious. Cushing shook their hands and thanked them profusely. The Polish doctor long ago had said he feared there were no miracles, and this was clearly what he meant, he knew that now. And he knew his wife would need constant medical assistance for the short, precious time she had left.

He arranged day and night care, and rang his agent to cancel his role in the *Mummy* picture they'd started shooting. He was not irreplaceable. Other people in this life were.

Now he remembered the crew sending flowers to the funeral.

As families do, of course.

He remembered, too, sitting at her bedside, tears streaming down his face. "I've made mistakes. I've done things of which I have been entirely ashamed, foolish things... Yet through it all, you have been perfect. You forgave..."

"I told you so many times, my love," Helen had said. "I never wanted you to feel I possessed you. That was our bargain, remember? What I know doesn't hurt me, so why on earth should it hurt you? It's unimportant. Those things simply didn't happen. You hear?" She'd wiped his cheeks with a corner of the bed sheet. "Not a person in the world could have done for me what you have done... But I'm tired, my darling... I can't talk now..."

In the bedroom now, all alone, he took the crucifix Helen wore from the jewellery box in front of the vanity mirror where she would put on her make-up every morning.

He placed it deep in the hip pocket of the Edwardian tweed suit made for him by Hatchard's, the outfitter in the High Street. It was where he bought most of his traditional clothes: caps, cravats, gloves. They knew what he liked there and never let him down. People didn't let him down, that was the remarkable thing in life. He remembered wearing this, his own suit, when filming *I, Monster* with Chris Lee. Now he faced another Jekyll and Hyde, another beast hiding under the mask of normality. A clash with evil in which he could only, as ever, feign expertise. Fake it. But at least with the right tools. And in a costume that felt proper for the fight.

Downstairs, the scripts and letters he had trodden over to get in still lay on the mat inside the front door. He picked them up. Clutched them to his chest. They felt full and heavy. Full of words and ideas and powerful emotions, and his chest empty.

"What if I fail?"

She was as clear in his ear as she'd ever been in life.

You shall not fail, my darling... With faith, you cannot fail...

"What faith?"

He faced the closed door to the living room.

Your faith that Goodness is stronger than Evil. It's what you believe, isn't it? You always have.

"I know. But is that enough?"

You know it will be. It must be.

He turned the handle and pushed the door ajar.

The room was in darkness as he walked through it. He placed the scripts and cards on the bureau, adding to the pile. He looked at one envelope and held it between his thumb and forefinger. He recognised the handwriting. It was a friend.

So many friends. And yet...

Darling, never fear... You are the one good thing in a dark world... and I am with you...

"Helen..."

How could he be downhearted when countless individuals led their entire lives without finding a love even a fraction as powerful as the one he had found?

He picked up her photograph and pressed it to his lips.

***

Square and temple-like, it had gone the way of all flesh. Now mostly a bingo hall, The Oxford in Oxford Street was a piece of faded gentrification, a mere memory of past glory, a vision of empire slowly turning to decay, a senile relative barely cared for and shamefully unloved. All those things. He remembered being told, at some official council function or other, that the original cinema opened in 1912, long before talkies, even before he was born. Rebuilt in 1936 in Art Deco style by a local architect, the regenerated Oxford's first film show was Jack Hulbert in *Jack of All Trades*. Extraordinary to contemplate, looking at it now.

He trod out a cigarette on the pavement.

Behind glass, Ingrid Pitt's fearsome, fanged countenance loomed over a tombstone. *Beautiful temptress or bloodthirsty monster? She's the new horror from Hammer!* He noticed his own name amongst the other co-stars, George Cole and Kate O'Mara. Inevitably it brought back the letters of condolence he'd received from both of them. And the strangers who had done so, too. He thought it peculiar, yet immensely touching, that those who'd never even met his wife or himself personally would feel moved to make such a gesture. The foibles of the human heart were infinite, it seemed, at times. But that notion did more to give him a chill of apprehension than stiffen his nerves.

Inside, the carpet tiles were disastrously faded and the disinterested girl at the ticket booth barely old enough to be out of school. He did not need to say "upstairs" as he used to, because the seats in the stalls had been removed for bingo tables. Upstairs were the only seats left. With a clunk the ticket poked out and he took it.

"Excuse me for asking. Are you Peter Cushing's father?"

"No, my dear. I'm his grandfather."

In what used to be the circle the house lights were up and he had no difficulty finding his way to a middle seat, halfway back. As yet he was the only one there. He took off his scarf and whipped the dust off it before sitting. It was more threadbare than when he'd come last, but he couldn't blame the owners. Trade was dwindling. The goggle box in the corner was sucking audiences away from cinemas: not that he should complain— there was a time, at the height of his success in that medium, when people joked that a television set was nothing so much as "Peter Cushing with knobs". But now people were becoming inert and frighteningly passive, like the drones predicted in *Nineteen Eighty-Four*, which so horrified when he starred as Winston Smith in the BBC production in the fifties that it caused a storm of outrage. Questions were raised in Parliament, no less: the remarkable power of drama to jolt and shock from complacency. Some outrage was necessary, he also considered, when picture palaces like this, almost jokily resplendent in Egyptian Dynastic glamour, were becoming as decrepit as castle ruins.

He thought again of Orwell's masterpiece and wonderful Helen standing just off camera, her radiant smile giving him a boost of confidence to overcome his chronic nerves. What had been the play's theme? Love. And what was the ghastly phrase of the dictatorship? *Love crime.* Two words that were anathema in juxtaposition. Except, perhaps, in a court of law. Indeed, he wondered if this was his own 'Room 101' in which he had to face the very thing he feared most: love, not as something sacred, but as something unspeakably profane.

His stomach curdled—as it often did of late—and he tried to shift his musings elsewhere. To Wally the projectionist, who once proudly showed him his domain, with its two 1930s projectors that used so much oil that, when it came out the other end, he'd use it in his car.

Cushing took his coat from the seat next to him and folded it over the one in front. He was hoping the vacant seat would be occupied. Eventually, if not sooner. For now he had best try to endure the sticky smell of popcorn and Kia-Ora embedded in the surroundings.

He put on his white cotton glove and lit a cigarette. Before he'd finished it Russ Conway's 'Donkey Serenade' faded and the house lights went down.

Without the pre-amble of advertisements, often the case in a matinee, sickly green lettering was cast over the rippling curtains as they creaked begrudgingly open. Mis-timed as ever.

An American International/Hammer Films Production.

Ah yes.

Jimmy ringing him in a panic saying AIP were getting cold feet because they'd cast an unknown in the lead, and a Polish girl at that. They'd already had to defend their decision to the Ministry of Labour, for God's sake: now the Americans had said they'd feel more secure with a "traditional Hammer cast". And so he'd stepped into the breach at the last minute to save Hammer's bacon. He could hardly believe that only a year ago he was filming it all on Stage Two and at Moor Park golf course, with Helen waiting for him at home, alive, when they called it a wrap.

He squinted as colour flecked the dark air and dust motes.

Lugubrious Douglas Wilmer's Baron von Hartog closes the book on his family history. He watches from a high window in the ruined tower of Karnstein castle as an apparition floats around the fog-swathed graveyard below. A phantasm in billowing shroud-cloth, the Evil not yet in human form...

The words of the actor in voice-over blended with the words Cushing recalled dimly from the script.

How the creature, driven by its wretched passion, takes a form by which to attract its victims...

How, compelled by their lust, they court their prey...

"Driven by their inhuman thirst—for blood..."

Cushing shifted in his seat. Why were cinema seats so desperately uncomfortable?

The camera tracks in towards a drunk who has staggered out of a tavern and stands urinating against a wall. His stupid face opens in a lascivious grin. Back inside the tavern, his scream chills the air and everyone freezes in horror—the way Hammer does best. The serving wench runs to the door and opens it to find the drunk with twin punctures in his neck. Lifeless, he falls...

Peter Cushing looked at his watch. Tricky to see in the dark. The merest glint of glass. Hopeless. Hearing the screech of a sword drawn from its scabbard, he lifted his eyes back to the screen.

Douglas Wilmer waits in the chapel for the apparition to return to its grave. As his eyes widen, the camera pans to a diaphanous shroud more like a sexy Carnaby Street nightgown than anything from the nineteenth century, and the naked, voluptuous figure beneath it. The camera rises to the face of a beautiful blonde. She steps closer and wraps her arms around the frightened, mesmerised Baron. When her cleavage presses against the crucifix hanging round his neck she recoils sharply, her lips pulled back in a feral snarl. Close up: bloody fangs bared in a lustrous, female mouth. With a single swipe of his sword he decapitates her. Moments later, her severed head lies bloody on the castle flag stones at his feet. The lush music of Harry Robinson, as romantic as it is eerie, wells up over the title sequence proper...

Still the seat beside Cushing remained empty. He lit a second cigarette. By now he was wondering if he would be sitting through the film alone. Perhaps his attempt to entice the creature hadn't been as clever as he'd thought.

The pastiche Strauss made him cringe every time. He'd never been impressed by the tatty ballroom scene at the General's house. The Hammers were always done cheaply—the ingenuity and commitment of cast and crew papering over inadequate budgets—but now they were starting to *look* cheap. It worried and saddened him. Like seeing a fond acquaintance down on their uppers. Byronic Jon Finch looked heroic enough, he had to admit. He didn't look bad himself as a matter of fact, in that scarlet tunic and medals...

Peter Cushing as the General looks on, presiding over his party. He kisses the hand of the delightful Madeline Smith, bidding her and her father, George Cole, goodbye. Or rather: "Auf wiedersehn."

Until we meet again. Obviously. The audience knows he will
appear later in the picture. He's one of the stars, after all.

He watched Dawn Addams as the Countess introduce her
daughter Mircalla, played with languid hunger by Ingrid Pitt—
plucked from her brief appearance in *Where Eagles Dare* after
Shirley Eaton (from *Goldfinger*) was deemed too old, even
though they were actually the same age. Perhaps Eaton, he
thought, simply hadn't given Jimmy Carreras what he wanted,
as Ingrid with her European eroticism undoubtedly had. Poor
Ingrid, who'd spent time with her family in a concentration
camp—("concentration camp: that's true horror")—and for
whom he'd organized a cake and champagne on the anniversary
of her father's birth: Helen had wheeled it onto the set and Ingrid
had blown out the candles with tears in her eyes.

*Peter Cushing asks the Countess if she would like to join in
the waltz. "Enchanted," comes her reply.*

"The invitation to the dance." A voice in reality: one he
recognised all too well.

Without turning his head, he saw the usherette's torch
hovering at the end of his row of seats. A silhouette moved closer,
given a flickering penumbra by the fidgeting and then departing
beam. The donkey jacket seemed almost to be bristly on the
shoulders, like the pelt of some large animal, especially with the
long, flesh-coloured hair running over its collar.

Eyes fixed on the screen, Cushing felt the weight of Les
Gledhill settle in the cinema seat beside him. He detected the
strong whiff of carbolic soap and Brut after shave, a multi-
pronged attack to cover the daily tang of blood and gutted fish.

*Jon Finch is waltzing with the General's niece, Laura, and
Ingrid—Mircalla—is looking over at them. Laura thinks she is
eyeing up her boyfriend but he says no, it's her she's looking at.
A sinister man enters the ballroom dressed in a black top hat and*

a red lined cloak. His face is unnaturally pale. He whispers to the Countess, who makes her apologies to the General. She has to go. Someone has died.

Peter Cushing as the General tells her, "It's my pleasure to look after your daughter, if you so wish."

Sitting beside him in the auditorium, Gledhill's face was entirely in darkness.

"Don't tell me you'll tear down the curtains and let in the light. You're not exactly as frisky as you were back in the fifties, are you?"

"I thought you didn't watch my films."

"Only when there's nothing better on. They're okay for a cheap laugh, I suppose. All they're good for nowadays." *The General says goodbye to the Countess and watches her depart in her coach. Ingrid stares out. The pale, cloaked man on horseback in the woods gives a malevolent grin, showing pointed fangs.* "Things have moved on, haven't you noticed? Blood and gore, all the rest of it. Nobody's scared of bats and castles and bolts through the neck." *Mircalla fondly places a laurel on the General's niece's head. Puts a friendly arm round the young girl's bare shoulders.* "They're just comedy. Nobody's afraid of you anymore."

Cushing chose not to point out that *their* Frankenstein's monster never had bolts through its neck. "I believe I still have a small but devoted following."

"I can see. We can hardly move for your adoring fans." The man he spoke to knew as well as he did that they were the only people in the audience. "They're dying, these old films. Everybody knows it. The last gasp. It's tragic."

"I think you'll find this film has been a box office hit. Significantly so, in fact. It's rejuvenated the company."

"Really. Look around you."

"You've got to remember it's already been released for five months. And this is a backwater town. And a matinee."

"You're living an illusion, mate."

"Am I?"

"You need to get a grip on reality, old feller. Before you lose it completely. Choc ice?"

Cushing imagined it was not a serious inquiry.

Peter Cushing's beautiful niece is sleeping now. Swooning in some kind of 'wet dream'—if that was the expression. He remembered that this was one of the many scenes that Trevelyan and Audrey Field, who had been campaigning against Hammer for decades, were unhappy about, even with an X certificate. The censor had strongly urged the producers to keep the film "within reasonable grounds"—meaning the combination of blood and nudity, the very thing Carreras was gleeful about now they'd entered the seventies ("The gloves are off! We can show anything!"). *In monochrome a hideous creature crawls up the bed. Wolf-like eyes out of blackness become Ingrid Pitt's—Mircalla's.* To Cushing the girl looks as though she has a bearskin rug crawling over her. Nevertheless, the dream orgasm so worrisome to the BBFC is curtailed with her scream.

"You saw the bitch," Gledhill said in the gloom. "What did she say? You know she's a liar."

"There seem to be an extraordinary number of liars in your life, Mr Gledhill."

Peter Cushing and an elderly housekeeper run in and calm Laura down. They say it was a nightmare, that's all. He kisses her forehead and they leave the room. They think of checking on Mircalla, but when they knock there is no answer. They presume she's sleeping. But the bedroom is empty. Ingrid Pitt is outside under moonlight looking up at the window...

"I thought she seemed perfectly charming," Cushing said, his eyes not straying from the screen. He pretended that it absorbed his attention. "Another woman with another boy who perhaps doesn't dream of vampires, like Carl, but of another kind of... creature of the night."

His companion remained silent. He found it uncommonly difficult to deliver the lines he'd prepared in his head.

"She told me you'd invariably take him off to bed, rather than her. That you'd spend time reading him stories, as a doting father should. Quite rightly. Your, ah, *special time* you called it, I believe... I wonder what your son might call it?"

"Now you are starting to bother me, old man."

"I'm rather glad about that."

The Doctor, played by reliable old Ferdy Mayne, tells Peter Cushing that his niece just needs some iron to improve her blood. Cut to Ingrid Pitt at the girl's bedside. Laura tells her she doesn't want her to leave. Ingrid lowers her head and touches her lips to the girl's breast...

"What are you going to do? Organize a torchlight parade of peasants to storm up to the Transylvanian castle, beating at the gates?"

Peter Cushing tells a visiting Jon Finch that his niece doesn't want to see anyone but Mircalla.

For a moment Cushing was taken aback by his own close-up. In spite of the make-up he looked tremendously ill. Of course he knew the reason. It was the toll of Helen's illness, even then. He could see the strain in his eyes. But it was a shock to see it now, thirty feet across, vast, on display for the entire public to see. He'd been oblivious to it at the time. He'd had other preoccupations. Now it hit him like a blow and it took a second for him to steady his nerve, as he knew he must.

"You think you're safe because you consider everyone to be as selfish and self-interested as yourself." Cushing did not look at the other man as he lit another cigarette. A scream rang out: the General's niece, after another nocturnal visitation. "You really are unable to contemplate that someone might act totally for the benefit of another human being, even though they themselves might suffer. And that's where you're misguided, and wrong. That's precisely your undoing, you see."

"You obviously know me better than I know myself."

"We shall see if I do."

"Shall we?" Mocking even his language now.

Peter Cushing's niece moans Mircalla's name in her delirium. He holds her hand. When Mircalla is discovered not in her room, he barks angrily at the maid to find her. Ingrid Pitt glides in, non-plussed, saying she couldn't sleep and went to the chapel to pray. She tells him bluntly—cruelly—that his niece is dead.

Cushing blew smoke and watched the horror ravaging his own face on celluloid, vividly reliving playing the scene, having to play it by imagining the devastating loss of one you love, and hating himself afterwards for doing so.

He cries out the name of "Laura! Laura!" Jon Finch rushes into the room with Ferdy Mayne, but no sooner has the stethoscope been pressed to her bare chest than the Doctor sees the tell-tale bite mark, accompanied by a glissando of violins...

"Consider this," Cushing said. "If I talk to the police, yes, they might think I'm a crazy old man, they might think I'm guilty—that is a matter of supreme indifference to me, I assure you. But because of my so-called fame as an actor, *your* name will be in the *News of the World*, too, whether you like it or not. Before long the disreputable hacks will be rooting round in *your* past, talking to *your* wife, *your* past girlfriends, *your* other—yes, I'll say it—victims. And if some of them, if only one of them speaks... Sue... Your son... And I think they will. I think they'll *need* to... And, irrespective of what happens to me, you'll be seen for what you are." *The General's keening cries echo plaintively through the house, the camera pans across the graveyard of the Karnsteins...* "And Carl's mother will know exactly what kind of man she is intending to marry."

A peasant girl walks through the woods. She hears a cry. It's only a bird, but it spooks her. She runs. The camera pursues her like a predator through the trees. She drops her basket of apples.

"Have you thought about what *I'm* going to be saying about *you*?" Gledhill said.

"You're not listening to me. I don't care."

The peasant girl trips, falls—rolls through bracken and thorns—screams, as a woman's body descends over her...

"Don't you? What about *your* name? Your good name. Peter Cushing." If Gledhill smiled, the man next to him was happy not to see it. "Up there on a thousand posters. Like the one out in the foyer. Your name, *Peter Cushing*, rolling up at the end of hundreds of movies. *Peter Cushing*, the name you fought for so long to mean something, turned into dirt. Into scum. A name nobody'll speak any more, except in revulsion."

"My name is irrelevant." The old man did not tremble or take his eyes from the images projected by the beam of light passing over his head. He would not be wounded. He would not be harmed.

Gledhill turned his head to him. "Then what about your wife's name, dear boy? Because it's *her* name too, since you married her. *Helen Cushing.* Are you going to be happy to see *her* name dragged through the mud? Because I will. You know I will."

Cushing tried not to make his tension visible.

The gong sounds for dinner and Ingrid—Carmilla now—and Madeline Smith descend the staircase of George Cole's home in striking blue and red, Madeline looking coy and slightly embarrassed about what's just gone on in the bedroom.

"You can't hurt her and you can't hurt me," he said. "It's impossible. You see, she knows I'm here, and she's with me, even now."

"Oh dear..." Gledhill laughed in the cinema dark. "I think you're going a little bit mad, Peter Cushing. I think all those horror films have made you see horror everywhere."

The monochrome dream comes again, and this time it is Madeline Smith doing the screaming. Kate O'Mara, the governess, comes in. Another dream of cats. Or a real cat? "The trouble with this part of the world is they have too many fairy tales."

"Horror isn't everywhere," Cushing said. "But horror is somewhere, every day."

"*You* might believe that."

The man was trying to imply that there would be forces of doubt, powerful forces, to face in the battle ahead. Cushing knew full well there might be—but was undeterred.

"You think you have power. You think you're all-powerful. But you have no power, because you have to feel powerful by attacking little mites who can't fight back. You take their souls for one reason and one reason alone—because you can. And now you're frightened. I can tell. Even in the gloom of this cinema. Good. Excellent." Cushing smiled. "It's my job to frighten people. You could say I've made a career of it."

A shadow hand creeps along a wall. The peasant-girl's mouth opens for a scream but no scream comes. Cut to the exterior of the hovel—then it does. The mother finds her daughter lolling from her bed with two red holes in her neck. Cut to Carmilla— Ingrid Pitt—floating through the graveyard, her voluptuousness under the Carnaby Street negligée...

"Do you want me to suck you off?" Gledhill said.

Cushing could sense his own breathing like a hot whirlwind. Could feel the creaking rise and fall of his chest and hear the beat of his heart, everything about his body telling him to scream, but his brain telling him to remain calm.

"Is that what would make you happy, eh? Or a nice stiff cock up the arse? You look the type. Yeah. Actors. Cravat. Well-dressed. Oh, yeah. I know the type. It's written all over you. *Mate.*"

But this actor found, to his great surprise, he could not be offended. The splenetic assault was as ludicrous as it was desperate, and, strangely, it had the opposite effect than the one intended. The very force of the invective meant his enemy was on the ropes, and it made him feel—empowered.

"Are you trying to disgust me?"

"I *know* I disgust you," Gledhill snarled. "You think you're a wise old *cunt*, I know—but really you just want to *fuck* someone, or something, just like the rest of the human race. You look down on me from on high, but you're in the swamp with the rest of us."

Cushing was astonished that the bad language didn't hurt him any more. He was quite impervious to it.

"I've never judged you," he said. "My only concern is the boy."

Then he felt a coldness in the air and something icy and sharp pressed to his right cheek. He had felt Gledhill's arm snake round his shoulders like that of an eager lover and somehow knew instantly it was the stubby blade of the oyster knife.

"What if I cut off your balls and stuff them in your mouth? Would that shut you up, d'you think? Or is that too much blood? What do you think, even for an 'X'? Never get that past the *fucking* censor, would we, *dear boy*?"

The cold of the knife seemed to spread through Cushing's body. He felt it in his veins. He felt it numbing him inch by inch but remained still and becalmed. "When did you die?" Not even the slightest quaver in his voice. "In your heart, I mean?"

Madeline Smith and Ingrid Pitt are sitting in the shade because Ingrid finds the sunshine hurts her eyes. They see the peasant-girl's funeral moving sedately through the woods, the priest intoning the Agnus Dei. Full of rage and sadness, Ingrid hisses that she hates funerals. Madeline says the girl was so young. The village has had so much tragedy lately. Ingrid begs her to hold her. They embrace...

"Look, she needs affection." Gledhill nodded towards the characters on the screen. "And the young girl is only too happy to give it."

"The young girl is not herself. She's infected." The knife tip dug a V in his skin, rasping against the stubble, loud in his ear.

"What if she's like that deep down in her nature, and the other one has just awakened what she really is? Set her free?"

"That's probably exactly what a vampire might argue. But no-one becomes a monster willingly." The knife against his cheek did not move, but he felt it tremble.

Both men's eyes were glued unwillingly to the screen.

That night Madeline begs Ingrid not to leave her room. She never feels tired at night any more, only excited, she says. But so wretched during the day. She hasn't told anyone. Not everything. She can't. How the cat comes onto her bed. How she tries to scream as it stretches across her, warm and heavy. How she feels its fur in her mouth...

Both men stared.

Madeline Smith says it's like the life running out of her, blood being drawn, then she wakes, screaming. Ingrid Pitt unties the girl's night dress—poor Madeline told by the producer it was for the Japanese version, but there was no Japanese version—*and Ingrid pushes her back against the plump pillow. Her mouth is on the young girl's throat, then slides down to her young breasts.*

In close-up, Madeline's pretty eyes—poor child, Cushing remembered, a virgin, didn't know what lesbians were—*roll wide in simulated rapture...*

"How were you bitten? Infected?"

Gledhill pressed the blade harder, making the old man's head shy away. "Life. Life made me like this."

Cushing could not be sure whether he detected glee, sarcasm or resignation. "Others need not be hurt. The very ones who—"

"You think *I* haven't been hurt?" Gledhill spat through locked teeth. "I've been hurt in ways you can't even *fucking* imagine." He wiped spittle from his lips with the back of his free hand.

"That's what made you what you are." Cushing tried not to think of the knife any more, or the threats, or the obscenities. "You know that. And you know deep down the boy must suffer, because you suffered."

"Jesus Christ."

"Who was it?"

"Jesus fucking Christ..."

Gledhill snatched the oyster knife away from the old man's cheek, tossing it to his other hand and back, then plunging it dagger-like into the soft upholstery of the seat in front of him, tearing it back and forth, ripping the material, then slicing it across. The dramatic surges of the soundtrack seemed to accompany his action, and when he was finished he hunched forward, the oyster knife gripped in both fists between his knees, his forehead resting on the seat in front, his whole body shaking.

"Who?"

"Leave me. Go."

"I'm not going anywhere."

"You can fuck off."

"I'm quite aware I can."

"Why don't you then?"

Peter Cushing prised open the other man's fingers and gently took the knife from his fingers.

"Who?"

The pale man from the General's party appears. The cadaverous man in the red-lined cape stands in silhouette in the woods as if bearing witness to Gledhill's words.

"Someone who made me think I loved him. Someone who twisted me round his little finger." He sniffed. A mocking musicality came to his voice, lifting it, lightening it: a delusion. "I fell for his charms, you could say." He seemed fearful the bitterness in his words evoked no sympathy. "I have feelings too. Did have. Till he fucking ripped them out of me. Why the fuck am I telling you this?"

Madeline cries out. The house is in darkness. Kate O'Mara, the governess, runs in.

"I know you won't listen to me," Cushing said, "but... confess."

A wettish snort, not even a snigger, in reply. "Bless me father for I have sinned. You make a good priest."

"I have done."

Outside the door the two women look at each other knowingly. Kate goes into Carmilla's bedroom and turns down the lamp. In darkness Ingrid slips out of her dress. The moonlight outlines her naked form. Kate moves closer.

"All is not lost. Tell the police. Nothing can be worse than the Hell you're enduring now. Do it. For the sake of your immortal soul."

"Soul?" Now the sound through Gledhill's nose was more weary than dismissive. He sat up straight again in the cinema seat and shook his head. "No. No way. I can't. The boy... What would he think of me?"

"Dear God, man." Peter Cushing could not disguise his bewilderment. "What do you imagine he thinks of you *now*?"

The blurry vision of Carmilla enters Madeline's room. The vampire appears to be comforting her in her sickness. The young girl wonders if she'll live until her father comes home...

"He loves me," Gledhill said. "I know he does because he shows it. I never have to force him. He never says no. I never force him, ever."

The Doctor arrives saying Mr Morton asked him to look in on his daughter. Kate O'Mara tells him Madeline has been ill, but it's nothing to concern him.

"You know what they do in prison to people like me?"

Garlic flowers. Their antiseptic scent. Village gossip. The Doctor puts a cross round Madeline's neck.

"Sometimes..." Gledhill struggled to complete the sentence he had in mind. "Sometimes I..." He failed a second time.

Ingrid returns to the daughter's room. She sees the garlic flowers and crucifix and backs out fearfully.

The two men sat in silence facing the screen.

The Doctor rides through the woods, against unconvincing back-projection. His horse suddenly shies and he is thrown. Carmilla comes round the edge of the lake towards him. In a flurry of autumn leaves she wrestles with him and sinks her fangs into his neck.

Neither Gledhill nor Cushing spoke. It was almost as though they had come to watch a horror film, and nothing more.

George Cole rides for the Doctor, but runs into a coach carrying not only Peter Cushing but also Douglas Wilmer—somewhat aged by make-up since the decapitation prologue—a man The General says he has travelled miles to find. To George Cole's horror the dead body of the Doctor is on the back of the vehicle. Peter Cushing says: "Now I can tell you, and leave us if you wish. Our destination is Karnstein castle."

"What do you want me to do?" Gledhill said.

The great chords crash. The coach pulls up at their destination. Douglas Wilmer holds a lamp aloft.

"Primarily I don't want anything to hurt the boy further, in any way. Bringing in the police and the courts will most surely do that. Horribly. But I shall do that if you leave me no alternative."

"What do you want me to do?" Gledhill repeated.

Cushing said what had been in his heart all along, and begged that some sliver of humanity inside the man still might grasp the simplicity of it:

"Do what is right and good, for once."

"Good?"

Said more in genuine puzzlement than disdain.

"Vampires are intelligent beings, General. They know when the forces of good are arrayed against them."

"Save yourself, in the only way you can. Disappear. Turn to dust."

Carmilla is dragging Madeline down the stairs. She needs to take her with her. Kate O'Mara pleads with Ingrid Pitt to take her too. Ingrid sinks her teeth in Kate's neck. Madeline screams. Jon Finch leaps off his horse and bursts in. Ingrid sweeps his sword out of his hand and grabs him but he grabs a dagger tucked in his boot and holds it up in the shape of a cross. Ingrid backs away from it. He throws the knife. It passes right through her. Double exposure. She fades and is gone.

In the Karnstein graveyard the vampire hunters see the figure of Carmilla entering the ruins. They follow, led by Douglas Wilmer's lantern. The long cobwebby table is a nod to the first Hammer Dracula, *perhaps. One of them finds a necklace on the floor. Peter Cushing looks up. They've found the vampire's resting place.*

They lift the stone slab from the floor. Peter Cushing and George Cole carry the coffin into the chapel. Wearing black gloves, Peter Cushing rolls back the shroud. "I will do it." He takes off the gloves. George Cole kneels at the altar and prays. Peter Cushing takes the stake. Raises it in both hands. Thrusts it down into and through her chest. Back at the house, her victim cries out. Ingrid Pitt's eyes flash open, then close, as blood pools on her chest. It is over. But not over.

Peter Cushing says, "There's no other way."

He draws his sword. With it firmly in one hand, he lifts Ingrid Pitt up by the hair in her coffin. Cuts off her head in one swipe.

As George Cole utters a heartfelt prayer that their country is rid of such devils, Peter Cushing's General lowers the severed head into the coffin. And Carmilla's portrait on the castle wall, young and beautiful as she was long ago—in life—turns slowly to that of a decomposed and rotting skull.

***

Cushing turned his head and found the seat next to him empty.

As the cast list rolled up the screen, he stood and looked round an auditorium lit only by the spill from the projector beam. He shielded his eyes with the flat of his hand but it was clear nobody was present but himself.

He was still standing facing the small, square window of the projection room when the house lights faded up. He found himself even more clearly in a sea of empty seats. The smell of popcorn and Kia-Ora returned. This time he found it almost pleasant.

He walked into the sunlit foyer with one arm in his coat sleeve. A number of young couples were queuing for tickets for the next performance. One person noticed him and smiled. He raised a hand, not too ostentatiously, not wanting to draw attention to himself, then criss-crossed his scarf on his chest and dragged on the rest of his coat. Another few people arrived. Quite a healthy gathering for an early evening showing. He was pleased, in a subdued way, as if one of his children had done well at school, with little help from himself. The film *was* a hit, and as long as the public liked it, he wished it well.

He let the heavy door shut behind him. Even more than usually when he had seen a film in the afternoon, the sunlight came as a shock. It almost blinded him, but he was grateful for the warmth on his skin. He raised his chin and stood with his eyes closed for several minutes, and when he opened them, found it noticeably strange that there was not a single gull in the sky.

Ten minutes later he committed the oyster knife to the sea with a throw worthy of a fielder at the Oval.

***

When he arrived home at 3 Seaway Cottages he felt Helen's smile in the air immediately, like the most delicate and distinctive fragrance.

"Look." He lifted his hand up in front of his face. "I'm still shaking."

You were wonderful.

"Nonsense."

You are *wonderful, Peter.*

He felt a strange fluttering at the back of his throat and looked at the door to the living room but didn't open it.

"So are you, my love."

Suddenly he found he was ravenously hungry for the first time in he didn't know when.

In the kitchen he took two slices of bread and cooked cheese on toast under the grille, served with a generous dollop of HP sauce. His appetite undiminished, he made two more rounds, slightly burned, just the way he liked it.

That night he slept soundly, and without dreams.

***

He was woken early the following morning by the telephone ringing as if on a distant shore. He sat up in bed, body lifted as if by a crane, not particularly hurrying to do so. Recent events still had not returned fully to his consciousness. Images drifted. Feelings coagulated, some real, some imagined, all vague and irrepressible. His head was too thick with slumber to sort fact from fiction and he wondered if he was waking up or acting waking up. He needed a minute to think about that, if you'd be so kind. The telephone, impolitely, was still ringing with a persistence normally reserved for insects and small children. He slumped back onto the pillow, hoping to return to the land of Nod. The telephone had other ideas.

When it started to ring the third time he could ignore it no longer. He picked up the receiver, rubbing sleep from his eyes with his other hand. He recited the number, automatically.

"Peter?" A man's voice.

"Yes?"

"Did I wake you?" It was Derek Wake. Appropriately named, in this instance.

"No. Not at all." He was about to add that he'd answered because he thought it was perhaps Joyce ringing, but the Inspector interrupted his thoughts.

"I'm sorry, Peter, but I thought I'd better ring before you hear this on the jungle telegraph. I thought you might want to know. Les Gledhill died in a car accident last night, on the stretch of the M2 between Faversham and the junction with the A249 near Sittingbourne. There doesn't appear to have been any other vehicle involved, and there was no-one else in the car at the time." Having said this quickly without pausing, he suddenly stopped.

Cushing felt the silence looming and wished his head was clearer. An element of him wondered if he was still asleep.

Meanwhile he heard the detective's voice fill the gap with more words:

"His car left the carriageway. It was a head-on collision. He hit the central reservation, the barrier, span across into the hard shoulder. Complete write off. As I say, no other vehicle was involved. ...Peter?"

"Yes. I'm here."

He was awake now. Fully. But he did not know what to say.

He wondered if the policeman would ask him next why he was in conflict with Gledhill over some issue concerning his son, and probe more fully why exactly Gledhill had made accusations against him. If he might resurrect the questions he himself had asked during his visit to the station concerning a film story about child molestation. A film which, when examined more closely, would be seen to be a complete fabrication.

But Wake asked none of these things.

"He was dead on arrival at Canterbury Hospital. Died instantly. Appears to have been driving at very high speed, from the tyre marks. No witnesses. Whether he lost control for some reason, or did it on purpose, we don't know. These things happen. You don't often see them coming. Those close to the deceased, I mean..."

Disappear. Turn to dust...

What he'd meant was, go. Leave town. Go away. Not this. Then he remembered:

What do you want me to do?

Do what is right and good, for once.

Good?

Save yourself, in the only way you can.

Dear Lord...

Was Gledhill in his final moments thinking of his immortal soul? Had he simply decided to do something good, for once, as he'd been bidden, for someone other than himself? Or was suicide just what it often was, as Peter Cushing knew all too well, the act of a coward? A weak man's only escape from an unbearable future?

"Peter?"

He rubbed his eyes again. The room wasn't focusing, so he kept them shut. He was aware that the other man could hear his breathing down the telephone and was waiting for him to reply, so he spoke in as steady a voice as he could muster.

"Derek, can I ask you something, please?" he said with his eyes still closed. "I want you to do something. This is very important to me. I can't tell you why, but it is."

***

The hospital, the car park, the very sight of the building itself inevitably brought back memories of Helen, and he was ready for that. Mercifully, she hadn't passed away there, but during her long illness visits were all too frequent, and each time accompanied by a sense of immense dread, of what might be discovered, of what one, this time, might be told. He was surprised, then, that no such feelings asserted themselves. On the contrary, he felt calm, in fact unusually so. Plainly there was a world of difference between visiting the love of your life and—this.

Naturally Wake had questioned why he wanted to do it, and Cushing wondered how many other questions the policeman kept to himself, and for how long he would continue to do so. But in reply to the man's enquiries—clearly worried at a widower seeing a dead body so recently after the death of his wife—he could only reply honestly that he felt nothing.

"Peter, these places are cold and clinical. They breathe death."

"I assure you, dear boy. I'm perfectly fine."

As they walked along the antiseptic-smelling corridor Wake explained that the sister's expression 'Rose Cottage' was the euphemism often used by nursing staff when talking about the hospital mortuary. As they approached it Cushing thought of the roses he tended in his own garden, round his own front door. The roses Helen loved. He pictured himself snipping one off and handing it to her, as he did, on many an occasion. How she'd invariably reward him with a kiss on the cheek.

They'd done their best to take the curse off the viewing room, of course, but it was still a hospital room badly playing the part of a Chapel of Rest. They almost needn't have bothered. As the door opened it had the feel of a shrunken and poverty-stricken church hall. The floor was the same slightly-peeling linoleum as the corridor, the walls insalubrious teak, with cheap beading intended to simulate panelling, and curtains on one wall a deep navy blue, the only colour.

He'd had it explained to him that the post-mortem had been done and the body was now being stored there—presumably in one of those pull-out fridges—until the undertakers collected it. He removed his hat and stepped closer to the bed, bier, table, whatever it was called. He was all too aware that the actions he was going through were normally the province of the close family, even though Wake had told him Carl's mother had no desire to see the body of her boyfriend. Accordingly, in spite of all he knew about the dead man, he felt he should behave with respect.

At a nod from Wake, who remained at the door, the assistant moved forward and folded down the white sheet covering the face so that the head and shoulders were exposed. Cushing noticed the clean, fastidiously manicured hands before the man stood back.

In death, they say, we are all equal, he thought.

He looked down and saw that a white linen cravat was tucked round the corpse's neck. He reached over and touched its rim with his fingertips. The attendant took a step forward and was about to speak, but Wake raised his hand. The man stepped back.

Tugged down, the elastic of the linen cravat revealed a livid scar running round the circumference of Gledhill's neck, the twine stitches, heavy and harsh, still abundantly visible. Frankenstein stitches. Holes dug deep with thick needles like fish hooks into dead, unfeeling flesh.

"Impact would have killed him outright," Wake said. "The front of the car was like a concertina. Steering column went straight through his chest. No chance."

Cushing pictured himself as General Spielsdorf again, holding the stake over Carmilla's heart and shoving it down with every ounce of his strength. Blood pumping up, filling the cavity as her wild eyes stared in perplexed fury.

"Cigarette?"

Cushing shook his head. Wake lit one of his own and blew smoke. It drifted in front of Gledhill's cadaver like the mist in Karnstein castle graveyard.

"As if that wasn't enough, he was decapitated too. The force of the crash sent him right into the windscreen. They found his head thirty yards down the hard shoulder. Apparently it's not uncommon. Tell you what. I'd never be a motorway cop for all the tea in China."

Cushing saw himself lifting up the body of Ingrid Pitt by the hair. The silvery flash of his sword as it sliced through her throat.

"They've done a decent job."

He wasn't sure what the Inspector meant.

"After a real old mess like that. I mean, he looks at peace."

"Yes," Cushing said, gazing back at the figure on the bed and readjusting the white cravat to its former position. "I think he does."

He didn't know if it was the effect of chemicals used by the pathologist or the fluorescent lighting, but the man seemed years younger, as if, absurdly, all the sins had been lifted off him. His skin unblemished, his hair neatly combed as if by an insistent mother. He wondered what was strange and then realised that, for some mysterious reason, his beard had been shaved off. He seemed, in fact, for all the world, strangely like a child.

Cushing looked at the crucifix on the wall opposite—the room's only concession to decoration—and found himself, in an almost imperceptible gesture, making the sign of the cross over his own heart as he turned away.

As he reached the door he heard Wake's voice behind him.

"Have you got what you want?"

"Mm?"

He turned back. The assistant was covering Gledhill's face with the sheet, and Wake was standing beside him, ash gathering on his cigarette as he sucked it.

"For your research? I presume that's why you wanted to see the body."

"Yes." Cushing tweaked the front of his trilby between thumb and forefinger before placing it on his head. "Yes, I have."

**

On the way home many thoughts went through his mind, but the one he was left with as he opened the front door was that, earlier, that morning, as his hand had picked up the receiver, he had wanted it to be Joycie at the other end of the line. Much as he feared talking to her, it was a fear he had to face—no, *wanted* to face, and that evening after a supper of Heinz tomato soup he decided to take matters into his own hands, and ring her himself. He was absolutely sure it was what Helen would want him to do. No, what she would *expect* of him. Because it was right.

No sooner had he said her name, "Joycie", than they both wept.

Without hesitation he asked her to come back. Equally without hesitation, she agreed.

"I'm so sorry if I've been rude or inconsiderate..."

"No, sir. You've never been that. Never." He could hear her blowing her nose in a tissue. Soon he found himself doing the same.

"What a pair we are," he said. "Dear oh dear. I shall have to get more Kleenex tomorrow, shan't I? I think I need to order a truck-load."

She laughed, but it was tinged with the same kind of enfeebled anguish as his own. He wondered, as he often did, if he would hear his own laughter, proper laughter, that is, ever again.

"You see, Joycie, everywhere I see reminders of her. I can't help it. This room. Every room. Every street I walk. Every person I meet. It's simply unbearable, you see..."

"I know, sir."

"Do you forgive me?" he said.

And, before she could form an answer, they wept again, till the tissues ran out.

**

Facing the sea he heard the tick-tick-tick of the wheels of a pushbike approaching. His was an old black Triumph from Herbert's Cycles tending towards rust, with a shopping basket at the front, tethered to a bollard like an old and recalcitrant mare. The other, soon leaning against it, was one of these Raleigh 'Chopper' things (not hard to deduce as the word was emblazoned loudly on the frame) in virulent orange, with handlebars that swept up and back and an L-shaped reclining saddle like something out of *Easy Rider*.

The boy, sitting next to him and finishing a sherbet fountain through a glistening shoot of liquorice, said nothing for a while in the accompaniment of sea birds, then, when seemed remotely fitting, pronounced that the vehicle on display was a Mark 1 and had ten speeds. Cushing pointed with a crooked finger and said there was no attachment for a lamp, and the boy said he knew, and they were made like that. He said it was called a Chopper, which Cushing already knew but pretended he didn't and repeated the word, for all the world as if the emblazonment had been invisible. But the object was new and gleaming and admirable, and dispensing some wisdom since he could, he advised the boy to look after it. Possibly the boy looked at the scuffed, worn, weary Triumph and thought that was like an elephant telling a gazelle to lose weight. But he'd been brought up by his mother not to cheek his elders, not that that worried him a great deal when it was called for, but on this occasion he chose to hold his tongue and nodded, meaning he would look after it. Of course he would. He wanted it to look new and gleaming forever.

When the sherbet was finished the boy walked to the rubbish bin and dropped it in. When he sat back down he chewed the remains of the liquorice the way a yokel might chew a straw, moving it from one side of his mouth to the other along slightly-blackened lips.

"You look younger."

Cushing had almost forgotten he'd shaved for the first time in weeks. He rubbed his chin. Dr Terror's salt and pepper was gone.

"I have a painting in the attic."

"What does that mean?"

"Never mind. You'll find out when you're a bit older."

The boy frowned. "I hate it when grown-ups say that."

"So do I. Very much so. I'm sorry."

He looked at the boy and beckoned him closer. He took out a handkerchief and rolled it round his index finger. "Spit on it." Without considering the consequence, the boy did, trustingly, and Cushing used it to rub the liquorice stains from his lips while the boy's face scrunched up, an echo, the old man thought, of the infant he once was.

"How's your mum?" He folded the handkerchief away.

The reply was a shrug. "She cried a bit. She cried a lot, actually. I didn't." A show of resilience, sometimes stronger in the young. The show of it, anyway. "But I felt sorry for her. She's my mum."

"Naturally."

Cushing did not enquire further. Out at sea beyond the Isle of Sheppey, a cloud of gannets hovered halo-like over a fishing vessel.

"They say it was an accident," the boy said presently, with a secretive excitement in his voice. "But it wasn't an accident, was it? It was you."

"It doesn't matter. It happened. He's gone now. It's over."

"I know you can't say because it's secret, but it *was* you, wasn't it? Acting on my instructions as a Vampire Hunter? I knew you would. I *knew* you wouldn't let me down."

Cushing tugged on his white cotton glove and pulled down each finger in turn, then lit a cigarette and smoked it, eyes slitting.

"How do you feel now? That's the important thing."

The boy wondered about that as if he hadn't wondered about it until that very moment.

"You know what? It's funny. It's really weird. I feel a bit sad. I feel a bit like it's my fault because I asked you to. I know he was evil and that. I know that, and I know he deserved it and everything. I don't know..."

"It wasn't your fault, Carl." Would he ever truly believe that? "Look at me, Carl. Please." The boy faced the old man's pale blue, unblinking eyes and the old man took his hand. "When they choose people as a victim, it's not the victim's fault. It's their fault. You've got to remember that." Peter Cushing knew that now more than ever he needed to keep a steady gaze. "I'm the world expert, remember?"

The boy nodded and took his hand back.

"I know. No need to show off."

Cushing trembled a smile and looked back to sea.

Periodically flicking his ash to be taken by the breeze, he gazed down between the groynes and saw a man in his twenties wearing a cheesecloth shirt and canvas loons rolled up to just under the knee and curly hair bobbing as he ran in and out of the icy surf. A dollishly small girl with a bucket and spade was laughing at him and he chased her and scooped her up in his arms, turning her upside down.

"She doesn't like me saying it but I keep thinking about my real dad, my old dad," the boy said, prodding a discarded Wrigley's chewing gum wrapper with his shoe. "I keep thinking perhaps he'll get tired of his new woman in Margate and come back to us. One day, anyway. I know he said he didn't love my mum any more, but he must have loved her once, mustn't he? So he might love her again. You never know. How does love work anyway?"

Cushing could hear no voices, but saw a woman join the man and the toddler on the shingle. The wind tossed the woman's blonde hair over her face and the man combed it back with his fingers and kissed her.

"It's very complicated, as you'll learn, my friend. Very complicated—but in the end so terribly simple." He felt a tiny piece of grit in his eye and rubbed it with a finger. The taste of the tobacco had gone sour and he prodded the cigarette out on the sea wall.

"Do you have bad dreams any more? You see, I have to check the symptoms, just in case. Are you sleeping well?"

The boy nodded, staring at the ground.

"Good. Very good." The old man took off his glove, white finger by white finger. Carl was still staring at the concrete in front of him. "Remember if anything feels bad, if you are hurting, or worried... Anything you want to say—anything, you can say to your mother."

"She won't understand," the boy said without looking up, as a simple statement of fact. "She doesn't understand monsters."

The people on the beach were gone and the waves were coming in filling their footsteps. Sometimes it seemed full of footprints, criss-crossing this way and that, people, dogs, all on their little journeys, but if you waited long enough or came back the next day the people were always gone and the only consistent thing was the slope and evenness of the shore.

When Cushing put his single white glove back in his overcoat pocket he discovered something he'd forgotten. Something he'd put there before going to the Oxford to meet Gledhill. He took it out and looked at it in the palm of his hand.

Helen's crucifix.

Opening the thin gold chain into a circle he put it round the boy's neck and tucked the cross behind his scarf and inside his open-topped shirt. The boy did not move as the man did it, and did not move afterwards, imagining some necessity for respect or obedience in the matter, or recognising some similarity to the procedure of his mum straightening his tie, in addition daunted perhaps by the peculiarity of the tiny coldness of the crucifix against the warmth of his hairless chest.

"I want you to remember what I'm going to say to you. The love of the Lord is quite, quite infinite. In your darkest despair, though you may not think it, He is still looking over you. Never, ever forget that."

The boy thought a moment.

"Is he looking over *you*?"

Cushing had not expected that question, and found himself answering, as something of a surprise:

"Yes. Yes, I believe he is."

Then the boy appeared to remember something, something important, and dug into the pocket of his anorak. He produced a rolled-up magazine, unfurled it and thrust it in front of the man, who had to recoil slightly in order to focus his increasingly ancient eyes on it.

Claude Rains in his masked role as *The Phantom of the Opera* stared back at him. Garish lettering further promised the riches within: films featuring black cats, Ghidrah the three-headed monster, and *Horror of Dracula*—the US title of the first Hammer in the series. What he held in his hands was a lurid American film magazine called, in case of any doubt whatsoever in its remit, *Famous Monsters of Filmland*.

The boy reached over and flicked through until he found a double-page spread of black-and-white stills. He flattened it open and jabbed with his finger.

"Look. It's you."

Indeed it was.

Christopher Lee as the predatory Count, descending upon Melissa Stribling's Mina. Baring his fangs in a mouth covered with blood. Van Helsing—himself— alongside it, dressed in a Homburg hat and fur-collared coat.

"I can't read very well," the boy said. "But I like the pictures. The pictures are great. Who's Peter Cushing?"

Cushing looked at the younger man in the image before him.

"He's a person I pretend to be sometimes." He thumbed through the pages, touched immeasurably by the gift. "Is this for me?"

"What? *No.* I want it back. But I want you to sign it, because you're famous."

"Ah. Silly me."

Cushing thought of the close ups they'd filmed of him so many years before, reacting to the disintegration of the vampire whilst nothing was there in front of him. He thought of Phil Leakey and Syd Pearson, make-up and special effects, labouring away on the last day of shooting to achieve the purifying effect of the dawning sun. He thought of the sun, and of the perpetual darkness he had lived in since Helen had died.

He lay the *Famous Monsters* magazine on the sea wall between them, took out his fountain pen from his inside pocket, shook it, and wrote *Van Helsing* in large sweeping letters across the page, blowing on the blue ink till it was dry.

"Brilliant." The boy held it by his fingertips like a precious parchment and blew on it himself for good measure. "Now I'll be able to show people I met you. When I'm an old man with children of my own." He stood up and held out his hand.

Cushing shook it with a formality the boy clearly desired.

"Enjoy stories, Carl. Enjoy books and films. Enjoy your work. Enjoy life. Find someone to love. Cherish her..."

The boy nodded, but looked again at the signed picture in *Famous Monsters* as if he hadn't quite believed it the first time. The evidence confirmed, he pressed it to his chest, zipped it up securely inside his anorak, pulled up the hood and unchained his bike.

"Carl?" Cushing said. "Sometimes you can hide the hurt and pain, but there'll be a day you can talk about it with someone and be free. Perhaps a day when you'll forget what it was you were frightened of, and then you'll have conquered it, forever."

The young face looked back, half-in, half-out of the anorak hood, and nodded. Then he took the antler-sized handlebars and walked his Chopper back in the direction of the road and shops, another imperative on his mind, another game, idea, story, journey, in that way of boys, and of life.

As he tapped another talismanic cigarette against the packet, thinking of his own journey and footsteps filling with water as the tide came in, Cushing heard the tick-tick-tick stop, as if the boy had stopped, and he had. And he heard the cawing of seagulls, his nasty neighbours--The Ubiquitous, he called them— and heard a voice, the boy's voice, for the last time, behind him.

"Will you keep fighting monsters?"

His eyes fixed far off, where the sea met the sky, Peter Cushing had no difficulty saying:

"Always."

***

He sat in the forest dressed in black buckled shoes, cross-legged, a wide-brimmed black hat resting in his lap and the white, starched collar of a Puritan a stark contrast to the abiding blackness of his cape. Over in the clearing the bonfire was being constructed for the burning of the witch. The stake was being erected by Cockney men with sizeable beer bellies wearing jeans and T-shirts. The focus puller ran his tape measure from the camera lens. Art directors scattered handfuls of ash from buckets to give the surroundings a monochrome, 'blasted heath' quality. And so they were all at work, all doing their jobs, a well-oiled machine, while he waited, contemplating the density of the trees and smelling the pine needles. It was March now, and soon shoots of new growth would show in the layer of mulch and dead leaves and the cycle of life would continue.

Work was the only thing left now that made life pass in a faintly bearable fashion. As good old Sherlock Holmes said to Watson in *The Sign of Four*: "Work is the best antidote to sorrow", and the only antidote he himself saw to the devastation of losing Helen was to launch himself back into a gruelling schedule of films. It was the one thing he knew he *could* do, after all. As she kept reminding him. *It's your gift, my darling. Use it.* And the distraction of immersing oneself in other characters was an imperative, he now saw. A welcome refuge from reality.

The third assistant director brought a cup of tea, an apple and a plate of cheese from the catering truck to the chair with Peter Cushing's name on the back.

"Bless you."

Occasionally, very occasionally, that's what he did feel.

Blessed.

It was a blessing, mainly, to be back working with so many familiar faces. Yes, there were new ones, young and fresh, and of course that was good and healthy too. The young ones, who hadn't met him in person before, possibly didn't notice or remark that he had become sombre, withdrawn, fragile behind his unerring politeness and professionalism—it was the older ones who saw that, all too well. In the make-up mirror he had never looked so terribly gaunt and perhaps they imagined, charitably, it was part of his characterization as the cold, zealous Puritan, Gustav Weil. But it was nothing to do with the dark tone of the film, everything to do with the dark pall cast over his life.

Those who knew him, really knew him, acknowledged that a part of him had died two months ago.

Yet the un-dead lived on.

Here he was at Pinewood and Black Park in the company of vampire twins and a young, dynamic Count Karnstein so seethingly bestial-looking in the shape of Damien Thomas he might well snatch the reins from Christopher Lee and become the *Dracula* for a new generation. The third in the trilogy, this excursion was being trumpeted loudly by the company as Peter Cushing's return to the Hammer fold. Once more written by Tudor Gates, heavily influenced by Vincent Price's *Witchfinder General*, it was the tale of a vampire-hunting posse with Peter Cushing at its head. And with top billing.

He remembered clearly the lunch a month earlier with his agent, John Redway, and the leather-jacketed young director John Hough at L'Aperitif restaurant in Brown's Hotel, Mayfair.

"You're returning to combat evil, Peter," the director had said. But he wanted a darker tone. He didn't want it to be a fairy tale like other Hammers. He wanted to reinvent the horror genre.

Cushing had said nothing as he listened, but thought the genre didn't need reinventing. The genre was doing very well as it was, thank you very much. He did think the idea was original, however, and the director had convinced him over three courses and wine of his intention to make it as a bleak morality play, manipulating the audience's expectation of good and evil by having them side with the vampires against the pious austerity of Gustav Weil, the twisted, God-fearing witch-hunter, uncle to the vampire twins, Frieda and Maria, played by the pretty Collinson sisters—Maltese girls whose claim to fame was being the first identical twin centrefold for *Playboy*, in the title role. *Twins of Evil*—or was it called *Twins of Dracula* now, the American distributor's illogical and factually incorrect alternative?

"You see, Peter, real evil is not so easy to spot in real life," the director had said. "In real life, evil people look like you and me. We pass them in the street."

"Really?"

"Yes. And that's what I want to capture with this film. The nature of true evil."

Whether it would be a success or not Cushing couldn't know. He would do his best. He always did. He had an inkling how this sort of film worked after all these years and that's what he would bring to the proceedings. That's what they were paying for. That and, of course, his name.

His name.

He remembered the conversation in the dark of the Oxford cinema.

According to the Fount of All Knowledge, Carl's mother moved to Salisbury shortly after Gledhill died, to live with her sister and set up a shop together. He hoped for once the gossip contained some semblance of accuracy. If she sought to rebuild her life afresh, that could only be a good thing. For her, and the boy.

For himself, there were other films on the horizon. He'd told John Redway to turn nothing down. He'd read the script of *Dracula: Chelsea* and it was rather good. He was looking forward to playing not only Lorrimer Van Helsing in the present day, but also his grandfather, in a startling opening flashback, fighting Christopher Lee on the back of a hurtling, out of control stagecoach before impaling him with a broken cartwheel. And if that was a success there were plans for other Draculas. Another treatment by Jimmy Sangster had been commissioned that he knew of, which boded well, and he hoped Michael Carreras would grasp the reins and take Hammer into a new era.

One of the more imminent offers was a role from Milton in his latest portmanteau movie *Tales from the Crypt*, but he didn't care for the part, a variation of *The Monkey's Paw*. Instead he'd asked if he could play the lonely, widowed old man, Grimsdyke, who returns from the grave to exact poetic justice on his persecutor. A crucial scene would require Grimsdyke to be talking to his beloved dead wife, and he planned to ask Milton if he'd mind if he used a photograph of Helen on the set. Then he could say, as he'd wished for many a long year, that they'd finally made a film together.

As it was, her photograph was never far away. He kept one above his writing desk at home, and another beside his mirror in his dressing room or make-up truck. At home he always set a place for her at the dinner table, and not a day went by when he didn't talk to her.

Hopefully there'd be other movies in the pipeline. They'd keep the wolf from the door and the dark thoughts at bay—ironic, given their subject matter. Not that he could see his grief becoming any less all-consuming with the passage of time. Time, as far as he could imagine, could do nothing to diminish the pain. The lines by Samuel Beckett often came to mind: "I can't go on, I must go on, I will go on," and he knew that the third AD would be back before too long, to say they were ready for him.

But for the next few minutes until that happened, he would rest and try to clear his mind as he always did before a take, and picked up his Boots cassette recorder from between his feet, put on the small earphones and closed his eyes. He pressed "Play". The beauty of Elgar's *Sospiri* gave way to Noel Coward singing 'If Love were All'.

One of Helen's favourites, and his own.

He had lost the one thing that made living real and joyful, the person who was his whole life, and without her there was no meaning or point any more. But what had others lost? Yet, they survived.

He pictured the boy on his bicycle riding away, the rolled up magazine in his pocket.

Whilst he was living, he knew, time would move inexorably onward and the attending loneliness would be beyond description, but the one thing that would keep him going was the absolute knowledge that he would be united with Helen again one day.

The spokes of the bicycle wheel turned, gathering speed, blurring.

Life must go on, yes, but in the end—*after* the end—life was not important, just pictures on a screen, absorbing for as long as they lasted, causing us to weep and laugh, perhaps, but when the images are gone we step out blinking into the light.

Until then he was called upon to be the champion of the forces of good. He would spear reanimated mummies through the chest. He would stare into the eyes of the Abominable Snowman. He would seek out the Gorgon. Fire silver bullets at werewolves. He would burn evil at the stake. He would brand them with crucifixes. He would halt windmills from turning. He would bring down a hammer and force a stake through their hearts and watch them disintegrate. He would hold them up by the hair and decapitate them with a single swipe.

He would be a monster hunter.

He would be Van Helsing for all who needed him, and all who loved him.

Afterword

by Mark Morris

I'll start, if I may, with a couple of first encounters.
I was ten or eleven years old when I saw my first proper adult
horror movie. It was almost certainly a Friday night, and my
parents had popped across the road to have a drink with the
neighbours. They had left my younger sister and me with a phone
number and strict instructions to call if anything *untoward*
occurred. I can't recall which of us decided to watch that night's
Appointment With Fear on ITV, but I remember the movie vividly.
It was *The Haunted House of Horror* directed by Michael
Armstrong. Made in 1970, it was a spooky old house/slasher flick
set in swinging London.

And it *terrified* me.

After the film was over I remember lying on the settee, literally
shaking with fear, unable to believe what I had just seen:

A woman hacked to bits! (In my mind's eye for *years*
afterwards I saw her blood-streaked hand crawling across the floor
like a crippled spider towards the candle she had dropped.) A man
stabbed in the groin and *blood* (!!) pouring out of his mouth!
(What awful anatomical connection had made *that* happen?)

Needless to say, *The Haunted House of Horror* made a
massive impression on me. I felt as though I'd been
unceremoniously introduced to a terrible, forbidden world of
degradation and madness and absolute savagery. It was a world
that fascinated and repelled me in equal measure. I was hungry to
see more, but at the same time I found the prospect of it
gut-churningly terrifying. Looking back on that time from my

present standpoint, I can still recall with absolute clarity that raw and intense dichotomy of emotions— that sense of desperately wanting to dip my toe back in to the water, and yet at the same time making myself almost sick with anxiety at the prospect of it.

Seminal though that experience might have been, however, it was, in retrospect, the *second* horror movie I saw (in my possibly erroneous memory this took place the following Friday) that had a more profound and enduring effect on me. That movie was *The Brides of Dracula* and it was my first experience of the wonder that is Hammer.

I recall watching *The Brides of Dracula* in a state of nervous tension. But whilst I was constantly on edge, I seem to remember that my initial reaction once the film had finished was one of relief that it hadn't bludgeoned my senses into terrified submission in the same way that *The Haunted House of Horror* had done the previous week. And yet, despite that, ultimately I found *The Brides of Dracula* more insidiously disturbing. Because whereas *The Haunted House of Horror* had been merely brutal, *The Brides of Dracula* was somehow… *wrong*.

By that, I mean that although the film was elegant, it had a sense of decadence about it, and was horribly perverse in a way I couldn't fully articulate. The fey, softly-spoken vampire seemed to me a creature of weird hungers, ones that— bafflingly for a pre-pubescent schoolboy—somehow intertwined sex and death, even a suggestion of incest, into one alarmingly potent cocktail.

What made the film emotionally bearable for me at the time, however – and even afterwards while it was weaving its strange, dark spell on my mind—was the symbol of calm and reassuring decency at its core. That decency was personified by one man; a man who not only stood steadfast against the sickening plague of vampirism, and ultimately defeated it, but who also led me, personally, through the movie and safely out the other side. That man was an actor who I had never knowingly encountered before, but who would, ultimately, become my—and is now also my daughter's—favourite actor of all time:

Peter Cushing.

Like many (most) horror movie aficionados of my generation, I can't fully express how much Peter Cushing means to me. Since that first adolescent encounter with him, he has been a constant and welcome presence in my life. Even now, as I write, he looks benignly down on me from mini-posters of *The Curse of Frankenstein* and (naturally) *The Brides of Dracula* framed on my study wall; numerous DVDs of his movies and TV appearances line my shelves; books by and about him stand shoulder to shoulder on my bookcases with tomes about Hammer and Amicus, the two movie studios who were his most frequent employers; I even own a hand puppet of Grimsdyke, the character he played in the Amicus movie, *Tales From The Crypt*.

Sadly I never met Cushing himself, but those who did never fail to speak of him with anything other than huge affection and incredible fondness. He was, by all accounts, both a gentleman and a gentle man—a man of impeccable manners, who never had a cross or unkind word to say about anyone.

The fact that he could convincingly play a whole variety of roles, from thoroughly decent, almost saintly good guys, like Van Helsing, to cold-hearted killers like Victor Frankenstein, is, of course, testament to his consummate acting abilities. Whatever role he was cast in, Cushing enriched and made wholly his own, and although he appeared in more than a few less than great films throughout his career, there is not a single instance where he doesn't imbue a movie with a touch of class simply by being in it.

It was in 1992, almost two decades after my initial acquaintance with the work of Peter Cushing, that I first became aware of Stephen Volk. Like millions of other people, I settled down to watch the BBC1 Halloween docu-drama, *Ghostwatch*, little imagining what an impact it would have.

I was subsequently both astonished and secretly delighted by the furore that the programme generated. As far as I was concerned, drama—especially if combined with 'horror', my chosen and beloved genre—*should* be provocative, confrontational, thought-provoking and emotionally unsettling. *Ghostwatch* had been all of these things, and I *loved* the fact that it had confused and frightened people, that it had rattled them out of their cosy little stupors. I remember thinking that I didn't know who Stephen Volk was, but that I liked the cut of his jib, and that from now on I would watch out for his name.

When his TV series *Afterlife* hit the screens several years later, I watched it avidly. If you haven't seen it, I recommend that you buy the DVDs and do so—it's brilliant. The very last episode, in particular, is one of the most emotionally affecting hours of TV drama I have ever seen. A sublime piece of writing, it somehow manages to encapsulate exactly what it means to be a human being, examining the nature of love and loss and mortality not only with an unflinching directness, but also with a tenderness and sensitivity rarely seen on TV.

Fast forward another year or so, to the 2007 World Horror Convention. That year's event was being held in Toronto, and my very good friend, Tim Lebbon, and I had arranged to fly out together. When, a month or two before the flight, Tim mentioned not only that he knew Stephen Volk, but that he had persuaded him to attend the convention, and that he would, therefore, be flying out with us, I admit I was a little in awe. I was excited about meeting Steve, but because of his dauntingly impressive movie and TV credits—here was a man who had worked with Ken Russell and William Friedkin, for God's sake!—I expected him to be not only a debonair and sophisticated man of the world, but also hard-nosed, confident, super-professional, perhaps even somewhat cynical.

What I *didn't* expect— and I don't know why—was a man who was just as much of an excitable and enthusiastic fan of the genre as Tim and I were. What I *didn't* expect was a man who was both open and open-minded, unassuming, personable, sensitive, empathetic, respectful of the work and opinions of others, and who liked nothing better than relaxing with friends and having a good laugh. To say that Steve and I hit it off immediately is an understatement. As soon as we met I felt instantly at ease with him, and by the time we arrived in Toronto after a seven or eight hour flight, I felt as if I'd known him for *years*.

And now, less than five years later, I can quite honestly say that he is one of my best mates. We and our respective wives spend hugely enjoyable weekends at one another's houses, we communicate on an almost daily basis, and he's one of the small handful of people that I feel I can turn to when things aren't going so well, and with whom I can be totally honest—and I'm pretty sure that he feels the same about me.

We're also mutual admirers of one another's work, though that doesn't mean that we constantly tell each other how unreservedly wonderful the other's output is. If there's something that doesn't work for either of us, then we say so, knowing that it won't lead to resentment or bitterness. Despite his excellent pedigree, and his undoubted talent, Steve is just as insecure about his work as every other writer I know—which, in terms of his short stories and novellas, is perhaps not surprising when you consider that, after years of almost exclusively writing scripts, it is only comparatively recently that he has devoted more time to prose fiction.

In my opinion, however, he has absolutely nothing to worry about; the prose 'branch' of this wonderful genre of ours is all the richer for his input. Over the past few years Steve has produced a good number of excellent short stories (*31/10*, *After the Ape*, *In the Colosseum* and *White Butterflies* are the ones that spring most readily to mind as superb examples of his craft) and a novella, *Vardoger*, a waking nightmare which utilises that old horror trope, the evil doppelganger, to great effect.

And now you are lucky enough to hold in your hands what I believe is not only his longest, but also his best piece of prose work to date. I was enormously flattered and honoured when Steve asked me to write the Afterword to his 'Peter Cushing novella', *Whitstable*, though I admit that I felt a little anxious too. What if I didn't like it? What if I didn't find it a fitting tribute to Peter Cushing? What if I felt that Steve had been unable to capture the great man's essence and personality?

I needn't have worried, because I honestly, hand on heart, believe that *Whitstable* is a truly wonderful piece of work—one, in fact, which deserves to win awards. Not only is it a beautifully sensitive and utterly convincing evocation of Peter Cushing at a specific moment in his life—namely the days and weeks following the death of his beloved wife —it is also an incredibly clever, moving and compelling *story* in its own right.

The skill with which the luridly melodramatic depiction of evil in Hammer movie *The Vampire Lovers* is paralleled with the grubby banality and far more complex psychology of evil in the real world is absolutely masterful. Similarly, both the close parallels and the colossal differences between the dashing and energetic Van Helsing, portrayed by Cushing on screen, and the shattered, grief-stricken, emaciated old man that he became after Helen's death is touchingly and exquisitely realised. What comes across most evocatively in this instance, I think, is the author's deep love and respect for both the actor and the man, and the inference that, regardless of whether he was playing a role or simply being himself, Peter Cushing was a hero in the truest sense of the word.

As well as being a riveting story and a deeply affectionate, note-perfect characterisation of a legendary actor, *Whitstable* is also a raw and uncompromising study of absolute love and devotion, and irrevocable, devastating loss. Helen Cushing died in 1971, and from that moment until his own death twenty-three years later, Peter wanted nothing more than to be reunited with his wife. He grieved for her constantly, and in 1986 even arranged for a rose to be named after her. The still-surviving film footage of Peter Cushing choosing and naming the Helen Cushing Rose is intensely moving.

Peter Cushing later admitted that he did contemplate suicide several times after Helen's death, but resisted the temptation not only because—thoughtful as ever—he didn't think it fair to leave someone else to clear up the grisly mess, but also because in her last letter to him, Helen had urged him to live life to the full in the sure promise that eventually, when God willed it, they would be reunited. Peter took her words to heart, and thank goodness he did, not only for his own sake, but for all the people —myself among them—whose lives have been enriched by many of the movies he made *after* 1971, personal favourites of which include *Tales From the Crypt*, *Fear in the Night*, *The Creeping Flesh*, *Asylum*, *From Beyond the Grave* and, of course, *Star Wars*.

All being well, the release of this novella should coincide with what would have been Peter Cushing's 100th birthday. I, for one, can't think of a more fitting tribute for one of Britain's most accomplished and well-loved actors than Stephen Volk's elegant and heartrending tale.

Acknowledgments

I could not have written this story without the precious local knowledge given me by Gordon Larkin, Brian Hadler, and Whitstable Museum.

It was also a rare gift to have the encouragement of Jonathan Rigby, Simon Kurt Unsworth and David Pirie (as well as their rigorous notes). Wayne Kinsey, Uwe Sommerlad and Tony Earnshaw all pointed me to crucial improvements, Charles Prepolec and Anne Billson drew my attention to some outstanding interviews, and John L. Probert and Thana Niveau shared a classic film I hadn't seen before. Thanks are also due to Tim Lebbon, Helen Marshall, Mark West, and especially to Mark Morris for providing a fitting Afterword, as I knew he would. I'm also indebted to Simon Marshall-Jones and Ben Baldwin for helping this project along its way.

Needless to say, Cushing's two volumes of memoir, *An Autobiography* and *Past Forgetting* were invaluable, as was a re-watching of the AIP/Hammer Films Production *The Vampire Lovers* (1970), directed by Roy Ward Baker from a screenplay by Harry Fine, Tudor Gates and Michael Style from the story "Carmilla" by Sheridan Le Fanu.

It is, of course, to "The Gentle Man of Horror", Saint Peter, this small volume of fiction is inadequately – but respectfully – dedicated.

Stephen Volk
Bradford on Avon,
February 2013
www.stephenvolk.net

Lightning Source UK Ltd.
Milton Keynes UK
UKOW05f1934161116
287848UK00023B/1171/P